PRAISE FOR THE HITCHHIKER IN PANAMA

"...the Hitchhiker in Panama will satisfy your cravings for romance and adventure. Alden weaves lived-in details about life on the ocean with a rich cast of characters that will whisk you away on a vacation without leaving your living room."

—Sara Whitney, RWA Golden Heart award finalist and author of the Tempt Me Series.

"The Hitchhiker in Panama is a delicious cocktail of sailing, wanderlust, exotic destinations, and steamy romance. Be warned: Once you step aboard, you may never want to leave!"

—Trish Doller, author of Float Plan

"If you are looking for heart flippy moments, a swoony hero and steamy love scenes go no further. You found it."

—The Romantiquarian

"I couldn't have asked for a better time for this story to come into my life. Travelling, sailing and the excitement of new adventures that I've been missing so much in the last year, all in one beautifully packaged story. Add some sweet (and spicy) romance into the mix and you've got The Hitchhiker in Panama."

—Kyra Parsi, author of In Love and War

"The setting is absolutely serene. You can feel it through the pages - the jungle, the sun and humidity and the sounds. It is escapist fun and just the story I needed to read right now."

—Literally Booked Solid

"This is a rollicking fun contemporary romance with an unlikely setting: a sailboat. Grab a pina colada and jump into this flirty summery read."

—Kristen Hanes, The Wayward Home

"A very real story of two people who have decided to live lives less normal but still facing choices of which adventure to follow. For once, a romance novel that feels real."

—Carolyn Shearlock, The Boat Galley

Have you read the prequel short story,
The Night in Lover's Bay?

Enjoy the first chance prequel between Marcella and Seb, a hot night of adventure in Antigua. You don't need to read the prequel to enjoy this novel, but it's a short and hot read. It's available to subscribers of my newsletter for free. Sign up and get your copy at lizalden.com.

Also by Liz Alden:

<u>The Love and Wanderlust Series</u>

The Night in Lover's Bay (prequel short story)

The Hitchhiker in Panama

The Sailor in Polynesia

The Second Chance in the Mediterranean

The Rival in South Africa (a novella in the *Hate Me Like You Mean It* anthology)

THE SECOND CHANCE IN THE MEDITERRANEAN

A LOVE AND WANDERLUST NOVEL

LIZ ALDEN

THE SECOND CHANCE IN THE MEDITERRANEAN

ISBN-13: 978-1-954705-06-7

First Edition

Library of Congress Control Number: 2021912710

League City, Texas, United States of America

Cover Design by E Stokes Creative

Developmental Editor: Tiffany Tyer

Copy Editor: Kaitlin Severini

Proofreader: Annette Szlachta

Sensitivity Reader: Stephanie Weber

To my readers.

Thank you for taking a chance on me and making this adventure fun.

ONE

FIVE AIRPORTS. THAT WAS HOW MANY I'D PASSED through in the last forty-eight hours, and the thought of trying to find a near-stranger in a busy airport was almost enough to make me sit down and cry.

I searched through the crowds in the terminal, looking for a face that should be vaguely familiar. The airport of Tivat, Montenegro, was small but modern, and I loved it simply because it was my final destination. I had already picked up my bags and was trying to navigate the crowds with a luggage cart, so that was an improvement. In Belgrade, my fourth airport of this trip, I'd forgotten where I was and had to ask an energetic business traveler what city I was in.

My face had been pressed to the window of the

airplane during our landing. Our plane had come in low over the Bay of Kotor, a huge body of water connected to the Adriatic Sea. The runway came right up to the edge of the bay, the surrounding land flat compared to the rugged mountains inland.

A sign caught my eye: "Marcella Baresi." The man holding it was in his late forties, with salt-and-pepper hair, very handsome—my new boss.

Dominic Morris's eyes connected with mine, and he gave me a friendly smile.

"Marcella," he said, letting the sign fall with one hand and offering me the other. "It's great to see you again." Dom was a Kiwi from Auckland, a sailing mecca, and had a breadth of experience that made mine insignificant. I wasn't much of a sailor, but Dom's credentials included qualifying for the Olympics, sailing in the Rolex Sydney Hobart Yacht Race, and participating in the America's Cup.

We met last year when I had been working as a chef on the superyacht *Odyssey* in Antigua. The owners of *Odyssey* had friends—Natasha and Justin Boyd—who were superyacht shopping, and they had already hired Dom as the captain to help in their search.

Dom, Natasha, and Justin had stayed only one night, but we'd made a huge event of it and I had impressed Natasha and Justin with my chef's degustation. Months later, when I looked for a position, they were in need of a new chef, and thanks to my superyacht crew connections, I was recommended for the job.

I shook his hand. "Thank you," I said. "I didn't expect you to pick me up yourself."

"Yeah, no worries. I like meeting new crew quickly and getting them settled in. Plus, I work the rest of the staff to the bone; at least I get to slog off and enjoy the nice drive." He winked.

Dom grabbed the handle of one of my bags and tossed it over his shoulder. "Right this way." I followed him out the airport doors, where the mid-June heat of the Mediterranean summer shocked me. He pointed us toward the parking lot. We loaded my things into the back of his car and pulled out, heading down to the waterfront.

"You flew in from . . .Tahiti, is that right?"

"Yes, I did." I closed my eyes and leaned back against the headrest. Though the scenery was beautiful, I was *exhausted*.

"Sweet as. That must have been beautiful. How many flights was that?"

I smiled at Dom's Kiwi-ism. I looked at the ceiling of the car and ticked off my fingers. "Tahiti to Vancouver to Paris to Belgrade to here. Four flights."

He gave a low whistle. "And you were crew on a private yacht?"

"Right. I was unpaid but still doing most of the cooking. Obviously, it's nothing like I did on *Odyssey* or will do here, but I also didn't work nearly as hard."

"You had time to get out and see the islands, hey? That part of the world is gorgeous."

"It is." I closed my eyes again, remembering the clear waters and idyllic beaches of French Polynesia.

"Are you sad to leave the boat? You were with them for a while."

"Sad, yes. It was a good crew and a lot of fun people; the adventure was amazing. But"—I shook my head—"my bank account is unhappy."

"Well, it's not over. You have a new kind of adventure now."

WE PULLED UP TO PORTO MONTENEGRO, A HUGE modern marina in Tivat. There were no skyscrapers here, just low-lying Mediterranean-style buildings with terra-cotta roofs. The marina was more modern, with a massive row of superyachts tied up. Each boat was backed up to the dock, and gangways were rolled out to allow for boarding onto the stern. *Themis* was different, though. The largest yacht in the marina, she was tied up on her side, a passerelle in the middle of her port beam. Her shiny navy-blue hull reflected the light and glimmered.

"Hey! Toby! Can you come help us?" Dom called.

The yacht was huge—I knew the specs from the job listing and I had done a bit of searching online for photos and videos, but nothing I had seen had done the boat justice. At nearly ninety meters, she was one of the largest sailing yachts in the world, probably the largest I would ever work on. Despite her length, she had only three decks, so she wasn't that tall, but her masts towered over everything else in the marina.

And she was a marvel to look at. Having spent the last few months on a sailboat, I was completely unprepared for how advanced and spaceship-like *Themis* looked. The way she was set up to sail was different from a normal sailboat, and while back on *Eik* I had been able to adjust the lines and pull out the sails myself, I had no clue where to even start with any of that on *Themis*. Thank God it wasn't in my job description.

There were plenty of people who were much better sailors than I. The yacht was staffed with more yachties than I'd ever worked with before too. Including myself, there were nineteen crew members aboard, and I could already see a few of them hard at work on deck.

At Dom's call, a young guy polishing stainless steel looked up and waved. He left his job and walked along the rail and down the ramp, meeting us at the base of the gangway and taking my bags from me.

"You must be Marcella, our new chef. Nice to meet you." Like the rest of the crew on the deck, he wore a standard casual yachtie uniform, knee-length khaki shorts, and a polo with *Themis*'s logo on the breast—the scales of justice over Grecian block letters.

"Hi, Toby."

I stopped at the pile of shoes—mostly flip-flops and boat shoes—on the dock, toed my flats off, and picked them up to carry them on board. On yachts—whether it was the seventeen-meter *Eik* or the ninety-meter *Themis*—shoes were not allowed in order to protect the soft teak or fiberglass decks.

Dom nudged his shoes off too and led me up the gangway. My bags were deposited to the side and Dom turned to me with his arms spread wide. "Welcome aboard *Themis,* one of the largest sailing superyachts in the world, and your new home."

Immediately we turned left and Dom led me down the deck. "I'll take you to your cabin first to get settled in." He checked his watch. "You might have time to nap, too. I'll come get you around four, then we'll do a quick tour of the boat and drop you off in the galley with Roy in time for dinner service."

"Thank you," I said gratefully. I would really need that nap.

"This is where most meals are served." Dom pointed at a large metallic table for twelve on the aft deck as we passed by. "There are service stations on either side of the deck and this is our bar."

My head swiveled every which way, trying to take everything in. The bar was circular, 360 degrees around. A track cut it in half, and sliding doors were hidden in the walls. The service stations, much like flight attendants had on a plane, were full of stainless-steel cabinetry and coffee machines.

Dom stepped into the stairway next to the service station. He pointed up. "To the bridge deck." But he took the stairs down. "This leads to our two cabins and the utilities area."

We passed through a small hallway. "My room, on the starboard side, yours on the port."

I stepped out of the way so Toby and two more

deckhands could step into my cabin and drop my bags on the floor. The room was small enough that I stayed in the hallway to give them space. In between the two was another small hallway and a closed door.

"What's through there?"

"Utility services like laundry and storage, and then beyond that is access to the below-deck storage. We've got a sailing dinghy, SeaBobs, eFoils, etcetera. All the fun things for charter guests. There are hatches on the main deck that open to give access too, but it's often easier to just pop through here."

The knob handle turned and the door creaked open, a familiar voice calling out, "Dom?"

"Seb? We're clear—you can come out." My heart skipped a beat. No way.

The door swung open and a familiar head popped up, wavy black curls looking unkempt, just as I remembered. His facial hair was a little bit more trimmed down than the last time I saw him, but it was still the same beard that had left my lips and the inside of my thighs red and tender for hours.

Seb smiled when he saw me, polite but a little wary, too. "Hey, Marce."

I was absolutely frozen. How had I not known that Seb was working aboard *Themis* too? Dom and I had talked about that dinner he'd had aboard *Odyssey* during the interview, and he had mentioned trying to steal Henri, the engineer, away, but he had never mentioned that my former crewmate and lover, Sebastian Alvarez, would be working with me.

TWO

SEB CLOSED THE DOOR BEHIND HIM AND PUT HIS ARMS out for a hug. My mind panicked, and instead of hugging Seb—which was so tempting, knowing how delicious he smelled, even when working hard—I stuck out my hand for a handshake.

"Nice to meet you." My smile was too big, too fake. Seb's arms fell to his sides and his brow wrinkled in confusion.

"Um, I think you know each other from before? Seb used to work on *Odyssey* with you?" Dom sounded confused, his voice a little bit higher.

"Right." I blushed, shaking Seb's hand. "I meant, good to see you. Seb. Obviously, I remember you." I laughed nervously and snatched my hand back.

Seb ran a hand through his hair and I watched too closely while his fingers slid through his dark mane and tugged at the ends. It was so shockingly familiar to see him do that.

"Right," I said, taking a tiny step away from Seb. The other deckhands had disappeared, and my bags were neatly stacked just inside the door of my cabin. "I'm going to unpack. See you later, Dom?"

Dom passed a look back at Seb but stepped away. "See you at four."

Taking deep breaths, I stood in the center of my room and tried to calm myself down. Seeing Seb here was shocking, and I couldn't imagine working with him every day. I flushed, thinking about my first day on the job at *Odyssey,* and how I'd accidentally walked in on him stepping out of the shower. My first few months of knowing him had been awkward, simply because I had the image of him naked burned into my mind. Everywhere I went on the yacht, Seb had been there with his infectious smile, scrubbing the decks, always seeming to be wet and shirtless. It wasn't until months later that I'd admitted my attraction—and we'd fallen into bed together.

But this was so much worse. Now I would see Seb and I would be thinking about the Time We Had Sex.

Also known as the Night Before I Got Fired.

I SHOULD HAVE EXPECTED IT, BUT A FEW MINUTES AFTER Dom left, while I stood in the room trying to talk myself out of a panic, there was a heavy, insistent knock on my door. It flew open, and Seb stormed into my room.

"What the hell was that, Marce? 'Nice to meet you'?"

I rounded on him and poked him in the chest with my finger. "'What the hell was that?'? What the hell are *you* doing here?"

Seb stared at me. "What do you mean, what am I doing here? I sent you the information about the job; you wouldn't have applied if I hadn't connected you with Dom!" His nostrils flared. "I recommended you for the job and this is how you treat me?"

"I didn't know you would be working here!" I roared.

"I told you, we were looking for a chef on my boat."

"No." I wagged my finger at him. "No." I grabbed my phone off the desk and quickly pulled up the last email that Seb had sent to me. "You said, and I quote: 'Marce, I hear you are looking for a job. *Themis* is hiring a chef. You might remember Captain Dom, who came to *Odyssey* for a night.'" I held my phone up to his face. "*Nothing* about you working here."

Seb's eyes started to show a hint of doubt. "I thought you knew I worked here."

"How would I know that? I've been floating around on a little sailboat in the middle of the South Pacific for a few months. I didn't have Wi-Fi most of the time!"

"Okay, okay, but seriously, it didn't come up in the interview? Dom didn't check to make sure it was okay with you?"

"Noooo!" I wailed. "I wouldn't have taken the job if I'd known you worked here. I thought it was weird enough that you'd recommended me."

His eyebrows came together in hurt. "You wouldn't have taken the job?"

I blew out a breath, frustrated. "Well, this isn't very smart, is it? We're already fighting and we have to work together. This is my dream job. *Porca puttana,*" I cursed. "I knew it was too good to be true."

Massaging my temples, I tried to figure out some options, but something tickled my mind. "Wait, did Dom ask you if it was okay?"

Seb shifted his eyes away from me. "Well, yeah. I figured I'd leave it up to you if you wanted to take the job or not."

"What . . . why . . ." I didn't even know where to start.

Hurt and then anger flashed in Seb's gaze. "Look, you up and left *Odyssey* the morning after we slept together and just sailed off." He gestured out to a hypothetical horizon. "I thought you'd moved on with your buddy."

I closed my eyes and tried to articulate my argument. "First of all, I hadn't 'moved on—'"

Seb cut me off, leaning into my space and frowning. "Oh really? I saw you sailing away with those guys. You looked awfully cozy to me."

"Excuse me! There was no 'cozy.'"

"He had his arm around you!"

"Okay, I don't know which one you're talking about"—he scoffed in disbelief—"but I wasn't with either of them. Jonas and Eivind are like younger brothers to me. I was upset to be leaving!"

"Well, maybe you should have thought about that before you left." And with that parting shot, Seb stomped out of my cabin.

I sunk onto the edge of my bed. Sure, I had been forced to leave *Odyssey* and hadn't even gotten to say goodbye to him. But Seb had kept his job, and how dare he treat me like it was my fault.

THREE

After Seb stormed out, I spent a few minutes poking around and half-heartedly unpacking. As the head chef, I had my own cabin. Dom's was probably a mirror image of mine. The two rooms were bigger than most crew cabins were, a privilege of our positions. That being said, my cabin was still tiny, especially when I thought of my childhood bedroom back in my parents' almond orchard in Italy.

There was a double bed set into an alcove, a big wardrobe, and a small desk. The head was through a doorway, with just enough room to stand in front of the sink in the corner, next to the toilet, and one step away from the shower.

Small, but all mine. I grinned, thinking back to *Eik,* where I had shared a bunk bed with Elayna and a bathroom with three people. I pulled out my phone, wanting to send a message to the crew of *Eik.* They knew about Seb, and I desperately needed someone to talk to, someone to ask for advice. But *Eik* was in French Polynesia, with limited internet connection. Or were they on their way to the Cook Islands already? I didn't know. I dejectedly tossed my phone onto my bed. I was on my own.

I washed off the stink of traveling in the shower and changed into my uniform, chef's pants and a crew T-shirt from the neat stack on a shelf in the wardrobe. It should have been easy to crash, but the excitement of arriving and the emotions of seeing Seb had washed away my exhaustion, and I had to force myself to lie down and try to sleep.

At four, Dom knocked on my door. I opened it, feeling a bit better after having gotten a power nap in.

"Ready for your tour?" Dom asked.

"Yes, don't let me get lost." I grabbed my chef's gear off my bed and followed Dom.

Two flights of stairs took us up to the bridge deck. Nerves fluttered in my stomach, and I realized Seb working here *was* going to be a problem. I was so worried about bumping into him again, and now we'd be stuck on a boat together 24/7. I swallowed, keeping my eyes on Dom. For now, I needed to pay attention to my boss, meet my new coworkers, and try not to get lost in this new maze. I'd deal with Seb later.

Dom turned to face me, walking slowly backward across the deck. "This is the aft of the bridge deck. It's really a patio for the VIP cabin." He hooked a thumb to his right, toward closed sliding glass doors. "But it's also private up here, with a great view down." He stopped in the hallway. "You should take a look."

I stepped to my right, toward the stern of the boat, and peered over the rail down onto the main deck. Directly below me was the dining table, and one of the massive masts rose in front of me. Beyond that were a half circle of couches and *Themis*'s tender at the very edge of the deck.

Dom opened the sliding glass door for me, and I followed him through a guest cabin and into a stairwell. "This is the atrium; the main way guests get down all three flights of stairs. And this"—he pushed open a door—"is the helm, aka my office."

Black leather, black finishings, black ceilings, and a 180-degree view of the front of *Themis*. If I thought the yacht looked like a spaceship before, the helm solidified it. This was straight out of *Star Trek*.

A cluster of people were huddled at one of the electronic pods filled with screens labeled with the B&G logo.

"Ah, this is Antonio, the best B&G technician in the entire Mediterranean—"

"World," Antonio corrected.

"Sorry, my apologies. Best B&G technician in the world. He's flown in to help us sort out a communication issue in the NMEA network."

I didn't know what the NMEA network was, and when I asked, Dom explained that it was how the electronics communicated with each other.

"And he's working with two of our crewmates here." Dom slapped a man on the back. "This is Gio, our first officer, my second in command."

Gio gave me a wide grin and shook my hand. "Welcome aboard." As first officer, Gio oversaw the exterior team of deckhands.

Dom leaned in. "Gio is also from Italia, but from Rome. He's a big Roma fan."

Gio crossed his arms and leaned back against the edge of the counter. "You are from Campania?"

"Yes, but I am not a big Napoli fan, so I don't think we have to worry about football rivalries."

Antonio cleared his throat.

"Ah yes, moving on, this here is Edie, our engineer. Hopefully you shouldn't have any equipment problems down below, but should you, she's the one to talk to."

Edie was petite and about my age, with a pale

complexion and bright eyes. The technical side of superyachts, captains, engineers, and the exterior team were typically dominated by men. She was a rarity.

We shook hands. "Pleasure," said Edie, with a strong British accent.

"Are you a Brit?" I asked.

"That's right."

"I studied in London. Whereabouts are you from?"

"Suffolk, but I worked mostly up in Dartmouth."

"Great, well, nice to meet you both," I said.

Antonio hacked, and Dom grinned at the old man. "Time to move along, let you fellas get back to work."

We took the atrium down a flight to the main deck, and Dom led me into a small office space and through another doorway.

"Now we're starting to get to the good stuff. This is the interior dining area. I'm sure you'll get pretty comfortable in here, though we usually have our meetings and most meals outside." The table was a modern monstrosity, massively made with metal, leather, and glass. It was empty, but there were chairs for twelve around it.

"Now, this here is pretty cool." Dom flipped a hidden switch on the wall, and I heard a whirring noise above me. I looked up to find a window covering opening up like a camera shutter, the spiraled edges pulling back. I could see all the way up through the ceiling, and straight up one of the masts to the clear blue sky.

"Wow!" I exclaimed. "Gorgeous."

"Just wait till you see it at night." He pressed the button again to close the oculus. "Then, over here." He moved to the forward wall of the dining room and pressed another switch. The wall opened, the opaque glass sliding away to reveal a climate-controlled wine cellar. "We have some of the owners' best collection housed here."

"Very cool. You mentioned in the interview that the chief stew is a sommelier?" My work prior to *Odyssey* was strictly in restaurants. I'd worked under Michelin-starred chefs and was hired for private events, but I was not as adept at wine as I was with food. It was especially helpful to me that the chief steward, the crew member who oversaw the stewards in the interior of the boat, specialized in wine.

"Catarina is, yes. She works with the Boyds' household sommelier, and she'll work with you, of course, to source wines and stock the boat. Fortunately, here in the Med, we have plenty of sources of excellent wines. There's another climate-controlled storage downstairs."

I nodded. Dom continued to show me more hidden panels and cabinets that revealed storage for the stews.

"How ya doin'?" Dom grinned at me.

"I make no guarantees that I won't get lost."

He laughed. "It's not too bad once you get used to it. It's only three decks, and you won't be up top much. Dinner service up here, galley and staff quarters down below."

"Only one flight of stairs—that's nice."

Dom barked a laugh. "All the stews love it. Much easier on the legs."

"My last superyacht was four flights, and once, one of the stews tripped going up the stairs and knocked out two others. They were unhurt, but unfortunately the desserts were trashed."

Dom winced. "Ah yeah, that's tough. This is your first run on a sailing superyacht, yeah?"

"Yes."

"Accidents happen a lot more often when we're sailing. Now, unsurprisingly, most charter guests don't have any interest in us actually sailing, but occasionally we do. And if the weather's good, anytime Nat and Justin are in, we go sailing."

Themis could be rented weekly for an ungodly amount. While I was sure superyacht owners in no way broke even, it helped them offset the costs of their yachts. Almost all superyachts chartered out, and that was where I came in. Feeding the owners, and feeding the guests.

"When are they planning on coming in next?"

"Three weeks. They fly in pretty often, so you'll get to know them well. And later next month we have the regatta, and they'll spend a weekend with us."

"Nice to hear they enjoy their boat often. Remind me about the regatta again?"

"Right, the Boyds' son, Alex, is a racer. While we do a couple of superyacht races every year with *Themis,* Alex races much more on smaller craft. Next month is one of those big races. It's in Malta, and *Themis* will be a spectator boat for day one, and then we'll host the awards ceremony the next night."

"And that'll be my big test, I'm guessing."

"Yes. Lots of fancy people to impress, high budget for food and decor. Basically, Natasha and Justin are using it to show off their new chef." He grinned. "No pressure, hey?"

"I've got some time to settle in. I'll be ready."

"Good." Dom nodded approvingly. "Shall we move along to the rest of the crew quarters?"

I followed behind Dom as he opened an inconspicuous door off the dining room. "We've got an upper crew lounge here." It was a small room with a dining booth and minimal counter space.

"It's basically a service station for the interior dining room and a separate cafeteria to fit all the crew for meals. Then we've got stairs down to your domain, the galley."

I stepped out of the stairwell and immediately to my left was my new galley, immaculate and shiny. I instantly fell in love.

FOUR

THREE WALLS OF THE ROOM WERE LINED WITH COUNTERS and appliances, while the center had a big island with cabinets overhead. I itched to start unpacking all my own personal gear, but I could instantly see the boat was well stocked already. I walked around the island, letting my hands run over the stainless-steel counters and functional cabinetry. The exterior walls had three big windows over the sink and counter.

Yacht chefs had to lose their vanity. The galleys we worked in weren't nearly as pretty as the big kitchens I'd enjoyed on land. Space was limited, and well, there were only two of us here to contend with. The galley was small, but I was confident it would be just right for our needs.

A tall blond man dressed in a chef's uniform

came around the corner, his jacket white with *Themis*'s logo embroidered in black on the breast and a few smudges from the day already.

"Ah, Roy," said Dom. "This is Marcella."

My crew chef. I gave Roy a big smile and a firm handshake. My job as head chef was mostly to cook for the charter guests and the Boyds, but Roy was responsible for the meals for the rest of the crew, and would also help me with prep work.

"Hey, welcome aboard," he said. I'd read Roy's CV prior to accepting the job, and had a refresher read on the flight over. Another Brit, Roy had worked in a variety of kitchens on the mainland before stepping into yachting.

"Thanks, Roy. Happy to be here."

"Want to give her the rest of the tour?" Dom asked Roy.

"Yeah, mate, someone's got to show her where our stuff is. You'll be no help."

"Can't fry an egg to save my life," Dom admitted. "Take Marcella over to her quarters when you're done here, yeah?"

We said goodbye and Dom stepped out of the crew area.

"Right, so," Roy started, "do you actually want me to give you a tour or should you just poke around and I'll hover annoyingly at your shoulder?"

I bit my lip and gazed in excitement at all the bells and whistles. "Yeah, you can hover."

I worked counterclockwise through the space, opening cabinets and poking my nose around. "How do you like the self-cookers?" I asked. *Themis* had two stacked on top of each other, an intriguing piece of kitchen technology that could steam, roast, and bake in one unit. I didn't have as much experience with them as I'd like, so I was going to have to be a quick study.

"Love 'em. I don't think I'll be able to go back to anything else."

When I opened up the cabinets, I found the spices immaculately stored in custom-labeled boxes. I raised an eyebrow at Roy, who was smug. "I may be a bit obsessive about keeping order."

There were specialty cookwares, like Thermomixes and Salamanders, and generous standards, like six hot plates and roll-out refrigerated drawers.

When I reached the other side of the kitchen, I peered down the hallway. Across from me was an open doorway and a room with cabinet space and two large booths. I looked back at Roy. "Crew mess?"

He nodded.

"What else is down here?"

"Crew cabins are down this hallway, and through this door are the guest cabins. After dinner service, I can walk you back to your room, show you the shortcut."

"Okay." I turned back to the galley.

"Right, so tonight's crew menu is street tacos." He pulled on a chef's jacket and an apron and I did the same. "You met everyone on your tour with Dom, right?"

"Most of the crew."

Roy showed me the folders where crew preference sheets were kept. "The street tacos are pretty easy. We'll dress some up traditional and some fusion, meats on the side because we've got the odd veg. And all the toppings go up here."

"Okay, sounds easy enough. What would you like me to do?" I asked Roy. It was a bit of a test. I would be working incredibly closely with Roy and we had to work out our dynamics as a team. Based on his past experiences, I was sure he'd be looking for a chef's job soon. I needed to know how we would get along. Would he be resentful of me because he wanted my job? Would he have trouble slipping between working as a team and being a subordinate?

"Can you make guacamole while I get the chicken going?"

Roy showed me where the ingredients and tools I needed were, and I started peeling and seeding avocados, putting the flesh into a bin for mashing later. Roy went to work trimming and prepping the chicken.

"So, where were you before this?" he asked me as we worked side by side.

"I flew in from Tahiti. I was on a small sailboat with some friends."

His eyes lit up. "Oh, like a vacation?"

"Not really. It was a proper sailing yacht. Seventeen meters, fully outfitted. I was on board for several months, sailing from Antigua to Tahiti."

"Shite, that's cool. So you know a bit about sailing, then?"

I shrugged. "Some. I mean, I could manage a little bit on my own. But this thing"—I waved my spoon around to encompass all of *Themis*—"this is insane."

"Yeah, it is." He tipped his chin up. "Those massive masts and sails, they're downright bizarre. It's like being on a spaceship or something."

I finished the last avocado and pulled out a knife to start dicing onions. "I take it you aren't a sailor?"

"Absolutely not. My family's never even set foot on a boat. But then again, they've also never set foot in a fine-dining establishment, so . . ."

I nodded in understanding. Money had always been tight growing up, so my family hadn't enjoyed fancy meals either.

"They don't get my job much at all. They definitely don't get how cool it is to be working on *Themis*. What about your family?"

"My parents live in Campania, near Naples."

"Were you one of those Italians who grew up in the kitchen with your granny making marinara sauce?" he teased.

"Actually . . ."

"Oh shite. You were, weren't you?"

"No, I was not." I gave him a teasing smile. "My parents own an almond orchard. I didn't grow up with my *nonna*'s marinara sauce, but I grew up with a little café and a store at the orchard. I started helping out when I was young, and eventually realized that there was a lot more to learn about cooking beyond the café."

"Then you went to culinary school?"

"You got it."

We heard the door above us open and footsteps thudded down the stairs. Seb rounded the corner coming down the staircase and hesitated a moment before giving me a nod and thumping Roy on the back.

"Hey, mate, howzit?" Roy said.

"Good." Seb leaned over and sniffed the chicken. "Smells great, as usual, man."

"What's up?"

"Running into town, thought I'd check to see if

you needed anything."

Roy glanced at me across the galley. "Marcella, you had some things you needed, right?"

I didn't look up from the cutting board. "Yeah, but I'll handle it tomorrow morning between meals."

"Okay then." Seb paused for a moment, and I felt my back tense up. *Please do not let him say anything untoward.*

After an awkward moment, Seb rapped his knuckles on the counter. "Okay," he said again. "Catch you at dinner." He strode past me on his way out. "Marce."

When Seb was gone, Roy glanced over at me. "Seb's my roommate."

I tried not to sigh. Of course Seb and Roy were roommates.

"We get on pretty well, so he's around a lot. I mean," Roy said, chuckling, "not like there's anywhere else to be, since we're all on the same boat, but yeah."

I stiffened a bit. I wondered if Seb had told Roy our history. That could be complicated . . . especially for Roy. Stuck between his boss and his roommate, if things got nasty, would he save his job or his friendship? I hope it didn't come to that.

When I didn't say anything else, Roy continued. "He called you Marce. Do you know each other?"

That was a positive sign. "We worked together in the Caribbean."

"On *Odyssey*?"

I nodded.

"Ah man, he hated that job. He's been working so hard to rack up his sea time, you know? It's not unlike being a chef in some ways, trying to find the right experiences on your CV to get the job you want."

Seb wasn't alone in hating that job. The captain, Carl, had been difficult to work for, and a little cruel. Seb and I had talked—even bonded—over the fact that our jobs were dead ends. I was supposed to be cooking grand meals for charter guests while we hopped from island to island, and Seb was supposed to be racking up sea time to acquire his captain's license. Instead *Odyssey* had languished in Antigua, mismanaged by either Carl or the brokers who booked charter trips.

We kept up the conversation while we worked, Roy telling me about his home life in Bristol and asking me all kinds of questions about my previous work. He was easy to talk to, but he kept his eyes on his job, smiling down at his workstation and only sparing me a glance now and again.

When dinner was ready, we prepared a buffet on the island of the galley. We moved seamlessly around each other now, only occasionally having to stop when I didn't know where something was stored. Roy made the call on the intercom, notifying the rest of the crew.

They filtered in, loud and rambunctious, so different from the other boats I'd been on. *Eik* was small and tight-knit, like a family, while *Odyssey* had been uncomfortable and sparse—toward the end, we'd had only half the crew we normally would've kept. *Themis* was going to be something completely different, like a big family getting together for the holidays. I didn't even have my experiences back home to ground me. My family had always been small, just my parents and I, who worked themselves to the bone to keep the orchard afloat.

Roy and I stood in the galley as the yachties passed through the buffet line. The ones I hadn't met yet introduced themselves. Everyone joked with Roy, and he was obviously well-liked. There was a smattering of inside jokes that bounced around the crew, with lighthearted teasing.

Will, one of the stews I'd met earlier, who was in charge of bar service, pointed to a dish and looked at Roy. "Vegetarian chicken?"

"Vegetarian chicken," Roy confirmed, mirth in his eyes.

Seb passed through the line, fist-bumping Roy

and giving him a wide grin and some teasing. As soon as he saw me, though, his face fell.

"Chef," he stiffly acknowledged me.

The disdain rolled off him, and the room seemed to quiet by a few decibels. I hesitated to give a response. His "chef" was cold and impersonal, but I'd look like a tool if I called him "deckhand."

I crossed my arms over my chest and huffed. "Seb."

He moved down slightly, looking over the next serving platter full of tacos.

"Marcella made those ones," Roy said helpfully as Seb reached for the tongs.

Seb paused. He *fucking paused.*

We both looked at Roy, and he grinned, far too cheeky for someone putting fuel on the fire.

My eyes met Seb's and held for a moment before he dropped his gaze and grasped the tongs.

I relaxed—a fraction—and the noise around us picked back up again, the crew more rambunctious. Avoiding my eyes, Seb finished serving himself and climbed the stairs to the upper lounge, where most of the deckhands had gone.

"Chef." Roy gestured me toward the buffet. He watched me pick through the remaining food, though I had plenty of choices. Yachties worked up an appetite working all day, so the crew chef always made enough for seconds or thirds. I took a little bit of everything. This would be my first taste of Roy's work.

Of course, we had discussed my preference sheet too, and Roy's—I'd be cooking for him on his days off. Roy picked at his food, trying not to watch me eat but too distracted to really focus.

"Good job on the chicken. It's very tender. And I like your chimichurri sauce."

"Thanks." He smiled and turned more enthusiastically to his food. "Glad you like it."

I looked around the mess hall, glad for my first day. Even with Seb around, I could see myself fitting in here. The galley was perfect, the food was good. I just hoped that my other dream—traveling and seeing the world aboard *Themis*—would come to fruition.

FIVE

"THIS IS THE SHORTEST WAY BACK TO YOUR ROOM." After dinner service, Roy led me through a doorway into the guest hallway. He tapped his fingers along the walls on either side. "Two guest cabins on each side." We passed through the atrium again and into another cabin. "Big guest cabin here, his and hers bathrooms." I did the math—with the cabin on the bridge deck, that meant six cabins total.

We cut through a storage room, and there we were, back in the hall outside my cabin.

"Are you getting all settled in?" Roy said as I opened my cabin door and stepped in. He leaned against the doorjamb.

"Yes, thanks. A few more things to unpack and some items to shop for, but it's looking good."

Roy looked around and whistled. "Someday this

will be my cabin." He looked at me and flushed. "I mean, not this one. Just *a* cabin. A chef's cabin. Maybe not on this boat."

"That's okay, Roy. I get it. That's the dream, right?"

"Yeah," he said. "You want to switch rooms? I have a shorter walk, but you'd have a roommate."

I laughed. "No, thanks."

Roy made an *aw shucks* motion and we both grinned.

"Right then. Get some sleep, Marcella, and I'll see you in the morning. Welcome aboard *Themis*."

MY FIRST FULL DAY ON THE JOB AND I WAS UP EARLY. Roy and I worked together on breakfast, just like we had worked on dinner the night before, but after all the crew had come and gone—including Seb, who really just glared at me while grabbing a plate and going to eat in the smaller upstairs lounge—I let Roy handle cleanup on his own.

Dom and I sat down at one of the bigger tables and began an information dump. "Have you had a chance to look at the calendar for the next couple of months? It's not super busy, but as we've discussed, a few big things are coming up."

I nodded and we walked through the schedule. Next week things would really be kicking off for us with a one-week charter along the coast. Our schedule was moderate; Dom was generous, giving us time off between each event. If all went to plan, I'd have a day off in Split after the end of the charter. I couldn't stop smiling, and Dom laughed at my excitement.

Then we'd move to Corfu, one of the larger Greek isles, and Natasha and Justin would fly in for a long weekend—a weekend I was sure was planned to test my chops and see if we were truly compatible. A few weeks after that was the regatta. Having to work on a large-scale event like this so early was intimidating, and I asked Dom about the planning.

"Justin will talk you through it when they come into Corfu. I know you have experience cooking underway, at least on a smaller sailboat, but there will be some surprises here. It'll be a busy week for all of us with prep, execution, and cleaning."

"What will we do as the spectator boat on the first day?"

"We'll be out early in the morning. The Boyds have invited some of their closer friends to accompany them, plus there are course photographers and judges, and a limited number of tickets were sold to the public. We'll have fifty guests total. The second day of the regatta, Justin and Natasha will be on their friends' boat out on the racecourse, so you'll have the entire day to prepare for the evening's big event, and we're capping the guest list at a hundred people. Passed hors d'oeuvres and buffets. You can talk to Justin about any additional staffing needs you have."

"Good, okay."

Dom switched gears. "What are your intentions for today?"

"I'll be going over the preference sheets for the charter and starting the first drafts of the menu. Roy and I will be going around to the stores to pick up some of the smaller specialty items and to get the lay of the town. I'm meeting with the provisioning company this afternoon, or at least their rep here in Tivat."

"Sounds like a full day. Do you have any questions?"

I shook my head.

"Sweet as. Then I'll get out of your hair. I'll see you at the upper staff lunch. Don't hesitate to call me if you need help." We shook hands, and Dom left the crew lounge. I stacked all my paperwork and packed up my laptop before getting up to find Roy.

The galley was spotless and empty, but on the whiteboard there was a note.

Marcella, meet you at the stern at 10. —Roy

Below that, someone else had written:

"There is no sincerer love than the love of food." — George Bernard Shaw

I chuckled to myself. The love of food had gotten me here. In fact, it had gotten me to a lot of places. Seb aside, this job was full of promise. I couldn't wait to get started.

STEPPING OUT ONTO THE DECK OF *THEMIS,* I SHIELDED my eyes from the sun and looked around for the rest of the upper crew. Roy was serving lunch to the stews and deckhands downstairs, but Dom had organized a lunch outing for the management staff. I knew that it would be beyond just a team lunch—it was everyone getting to know me.

As soon as my eyes adjusted, my heart skipped a beat. It was like going back in time: Seb stood to the side of the deck, facing away from me, hose in one hand, sudsy brush in the other; he was shirtless, his tanned skin on display in the Mediterranean sun.

It was part of his job, I knew, but he had *always* been like this on *Odyssey,* and it was so hard to pull my eyes away. He'd gotten me into this mess—into so many messes—did he have to rub it in, really?

"God, put a shirt on," I muttered under my breath.

Too loudly apparently. The brush paused, and Seb turned around to glare at me. "This is my domain, not yours, Marce. You don't get to tell me how to do my job."

"I wasn't."

I should leave.

Seb dropped the brush and the hose, muffled *thunks* sounding as each hit the carpeted deck.

I really need to leave.

Gripping the rails on either side of him, Seb leaned back. Muscles jumped in his chest, his biceps stretched, and I was glad my sunglasses hid my eyes.

But he smirked anyway and my feet remained rooted to the floor.

"Marcella?" Cat's voice jerked me out of my frozen state and I spun around. Her gaze vacillated between me and Seb for a moment and I imagined her eyes bouncing back and forth behind her sunglasses. Seb and I were both incriminatingly quiet. I didn't know what to say—one day in and I'd already been caught ogling him.

"Are you ready to go?" she asked me. Catarina, or Cat, as she had introduced herself, was the chief stew. While I handled only my team of Roy, she had five stews who worked under her. Yesterday she'd been brief but friendly. It had been much appreciated. As chief stew, she was the crew member I'd work with most aside from Roy, and with that pressure and proximity, chefs and chief stews tended to butt heads.

Cat tilted her head toward the bottom of the gangway, where Dom, Edie, and Gio waited. "We're all ready," she said.

I tossed a brief glance back at Seb, who frowned at me. Was he upset we were caught? Or upset I was leaving?

I shook thoughts of Seb off and smiled at Cat. "Ready."

We took the ramp down together, and blissfully, she didn't bring up Seb. "Are you all settled into your cabin?"

"Yes, thanks, all squared away. It's nice to have my own room again."

"You were sharing a cabin before?"

I greeted the group on the dock and we walked toward the city center along the wharf. "I was actually on a private sailboat before this, a seventeen-meter sailboat as casual crew. I shared a crew cabin with another woman."

"Oh goodness. Was this a job or . . . ?"

I chuckled. "More of an adventure. I was at a bit of a dead-end job in the Caribbean and they offered me a chance to sail through some of the Caribbean islands and out through the Pacific."

"Ah, that's amazing. Didn't you just love it? I was a stew on a yacht in Fiji a few years ago, but it was just temp work."

"I didn't get that far, unfortunately, just around French Polynesia. But what I did see was amazing."

We compared notes over the islands as we trailed behind the rest of the group. Cat had an eastern European accent and a keen eye for details. And she had a great memory for things that had happened years previously.

Dom stepped aside to a small café with outdoor seating and we were led to one of the tables under an umbrella.

Menus were distributed and drink orders placed. I quickly picked out my lunch and put my menu back down. "Dom, when we first met, you were helping the Boyds shop. How did you end up picking out *Themis*?"

"Ah yeah. Natasha had her heart set on something big and really tech driven. She acquired most of her wealth through investing in various technologies, including some carbon fiber projects, so she was very attracted to *Themis* for its innovation. Beyond that, we just had pure luck that the ship came up for sale at the time."

"When was that purchase made?"

"About six months ago. Not that long after our dinner on *Odyssey.* The Wrights were a bit put out when Nat and Justin didn't listen to their advice on superyachts, I suppose. Doesn't help that the Boyds one-upped them."

Sweeping my fingers around the table, I asked the rest of the crew, "When did everyone join on?"

Cat waggled her fingers. "I'd worked with Dom before, so he snatched me up right away. Gave me an offer I couldn't refuse."

I shifted my attention to Edie, who closed her menu. "I came with *Themis;* I've been on board for a little over a year now."

"Ah, it's good to have an engineer who knows the boat so well, then."

She grinned at me. "Every nook and cranny."

"And I've been here about a month," Gio informed me. "I was placed through a yacht agency."

I nodded. I'd gotten the job on *Odyssey* through a yacht agency, so I knew how that went. Crystal had promised me it would be my dream job, when it was far from it. The experience had left a bitter taste in my mouth.

Edie tilted her head. "Dom told us you've been sailing?"

I explained the trip on *Eik* again, reinforcing that

Eik was nothing like *Themis* and the two boats weren't even remotely similar.

"I obviously searched on the internet for *Themis* before the interview and did a lot of reading about her and her design, but I don't remember any of it now."

"She's a pretty unique beast." Edie grinned with fondness. "Her square-shaped rigging is completely rare nowadays, so most sailors have never gotten a chance to sail on a yacht like her. We have to go through a lot of training with any new deck crew. And of course, for regattas, we fly in professional sailors. Although we have a few on the crew now who qualify."

"She's pretty fast, right?"

She shrugged modestly. "Wins a few regattas every year, but, honestly, there aren't many to compete in for superyachts, not like some of the smaller classes."

Appetizers came and Dom shifted the conversation to food. "I remember a lot of the food you made on *Odyssey;* that dinner was one of the best meals of my life."

I blushed. "Thank you."

"Tell us about your work experience. I've obviously seen your CV, but these guys haven't."

I told the team about attending culinary school in

London and working my way through a few top restaurants. I'd had a lot of luck over the years, even working in a small three-Michelin-starred place in France. I glazed over these facts, but emphasized my time on yachts. I knew that was what really mattered; I was a chef who could work independently and with a variety of foods.

"I know Roy has notes on your preferences, but what cuisine or dishes do you particularly like?" I asked the table.

Edie made a face. "Anything but pub food. Please, no fish-and-chips or curry."

"I spent some formative years in Singapore," Dom said. "I like almost all Asian cuisines, but street noodles are the best."

"Anything made by my nonna." Gio grinned.

That left Cat, who groaned. "I like pizza."

The table laughed. "So low-class, Cat," Edie teased. "Just dial up the local pizzeria for delivery and Cat's happy."

"Ah, you've got to get off the boat for that one. Wood-fired pizza." I sighed wistfully.

"Oh no." Cat shook her head. "I like the greasy American-style pizza. I actually went to uni in Chicago, so we're talking really greasy. And stuffed with meat."

"Good for hangovers," Gio chimed in.

Dom's phone rang on his hip and he checked the number. "Excuse me." He answered while walking away. "Diane?"

A collective groan went up around the table.

I looked from Cat's wrinkled nose to Gio's shaking head. "What? Who's Diane?"

"Dom's ex," Cat told me. "They split up years ago, but he's got two kids, and it's always been a difficult thing for him."

"And that"—Gio looked at me pointedly—"is why the rest of us are all firmly single."

"That and your looks," Edie teased, throwing a straw wrapper at Gio.

"I'm guessing you don't have anyone back home, Marcella?" Cat asked.

"No, no one back home."

The conversation moved on and I enjoyed getting to know my crewmates. Cat, with the exception of her pizza adoration, was a big foodie. We peppered the server with questions and compared notes on the food. She said that this year was her eighth season in the Mediterranean. She knew the ports well, and this was her fifth time in Tivat. The Adriatic Sea was getting to be a more popular destination for superyachts, and she claimed ritzy ports like Monaco and Nice were losing ground to the cheaper, trendier eastern ports.

The whole meal was like dinner the night before, loud, rambunctious, with lots of teasing and laughter. I wondered how long it would take for me to fit in like that or, with the tension between me and Seb, would I ever get there?

SIX

My first week had flown by. Every day was busy from dawn to dusk, planning out the menus for the upcoming charter week or helping Roy with crew meals. We were transitioning into a long-term, stable working relationship. Roy was deferring to me, accepting my suggestions, and asking for advice.

And I had met most of my vendors and had sources for everything on my list for the upcoming week. Roy and I had gone over the entire inventory and made sure the boat was well stocked. When I suggested a change in organization from how the past chef kept things, Roy took it in stride.

Thankfully, I had received messages from my friends on *Eik*—Jonas was including me in the regular email updates on their position, Lila had gleefully announced that her and Eivind's wedding was going to happen in New Zealand, and Elayna, my former roommate, had left *Eik* and sent me several long and winding emails, the kind filled with the existential crises of someone trying to find their place in the world. I wrote each of them back, and though messages were slow to be returned thanks to the vast time difference, it made me feel better—more settled.

As for Seb, hellos and thank-yous were the most words we had shared all week. We hadn't avoided each other, which would be impossible, even on a ninety-meter boat, but we'd barely talked when we were in the same room, which was surprisingly often.

Seb and Roy were very close for roommates. Instead of sitting in the lounge and eating, Seb often took his meals standing up and chatting with Roy while Roy cooked or cleaned. He was always popping in for snacks, and Roy was often setting aside something Seb might particularly like.

"You and Seb seem pretty close," I'd commented once, after an extended visit by Seb had the guys cracking up while I chiffonaded basil at the opposite end of the galley, ignored.

"Yeah, he has been a great roommate. Hard worker, funny. I think we're a good match because we have such different jobs. Normally I'm just bunked with the token male stew."

"Do Will and Percy bunk together?" Percy was another stew.

"Yeah. I've never worked on a boat with this many guys in the interior crew."

"And this many women in the exterior?" I asked.

"That too."

We hadn't talked about Seb much since then, but by the end of the week, my nerves were frayed. When I'd first met Seb and I'd seen him naked, it had constantly popped up into my mind: him stepping out of the shower, toweling off, droplets of water everywhere.

After that night in Antigua, though, now anytime Seb came through the galley, when he groaned while eating something delicious or closed his eyes or even when I saw his hands, I flashed back to our night together. Seb's noises echoed through my head, and these memories surfacing were making it hard for me to concentrate on anything when he was around.

After a week of this, I was frustrated, mentally and sexually.

I was almost done for the afternoon, and Roy and I had a break on the schedule. We were tidying up the galley, and Seb was on a break too, fifteen minutes in the afternoon to come inside and eat a snack. Depending on the day's chores, deckhands would spend a lot of time out in the sun and heat. Washing the boat, cleaning windows, and various other projects all burned a lot of calories, so most of the crew opted for afternoon snacks and Seb was enjoying some of our fresh pastries.

He stood next to the sink, leaning over to eat a *pain au chocolat,* letting the flaky crust fall into the sink. He groaned around the bite, laughed at something Roy said, and licked his lips.

Ugh, he had such great lips.

Seb turned and caught me staring. Roy was focused on his dishes and the story he was telling, but Seb's gaze lingered, and then his eyes narrowed, as if I were the interloper in my own kitchen!

Absolutely not. I had to nip this in the bud and Seb had to know this was my domain.

"Seb, can you take your snack into the crew lounge, please? You're getting crumbs everywhere and Roy is trying to work."

Seb froze, and his gaze flicked from me to Roy and back. He looked down at the sink. "I'm just getting crumbs on the dirty dishes, Marce. Roy's chugging through them; they'll be clean in no time."

"I'd prefer Marcella. And enough with the crumbs; go eat in the lounge like the rest of the crew."

Seb looked at Roy again, but I couldn't tell if Roy was looking down or if they communicated somehow. He didn't move.

I pitched my voice sharper. "Seb, seriously, out."

He shoved the rest of the pastry into his mouth and dusted off his hands over the sink. His cheeks puffing up as he tried to chew would have been comical any other time, but we were both flushed with anger. He tossed his hands out, palms up, and stormed out of the galley.

Huffing, I made my own noise by stomping across the galley to the laundry bin and taking off my apron and chef's coat. "Roy, you got the rest of cleanup?"

"Yes, ma'am."

"Good. I'm off. See you in an hour."

I needed to do something. Too wound up to take a nap, I contemplated exercising to blow off steam as I walked through the guest cabins and into my crew quarters. Would that help my agitation?

Closing the door to my room, I crossed over and set my notebook down. A hot shower sounded good, but then immediately my mind went to Seb again. Damn it.

As if I'd conjured him, my door flew open and Seb walked in.

My jaw dropped. "Excuse me, what the hell are you doing here?"

"What is your problem, Marce?"

"Marcella," I gritted out.

"Okay, *Marcella,* what is your problem?"

"You, Seb, you are the problem! You are always in my galley, and you're nothing but a . . . a . . . distraction!" I hurled the word at him like an insult and I could see it hit him like a physical punch. His jaw tightened, but there was also a bewildered look in his eyes.

Seb stormed out, slamming the door behind him. I leaned back against the wall, pressing my fingertips to my forehead. What was I thinking? Of all the insults to fling, I had to choose the one that Captain Carl had thrown out when he'd fired me, the one that was most true, revealing anger and vulnerability.

These thoughts hit me along with regret, but before I could process anything, the door banged open again and Seb was on me. He pinned me against the wall, fingers thrusting into my hair and the heat of his body oppressive. My fingers gripped his shirt, grounding me.

He growled. "You are goddamn right I'm a distraction. I'm the best distraction you'll ever have." There was a tiny pause, a moment where I could have pushed him away, forced my fingers to uncurl from his uniform. Instead they tightened. And then he kissed me, his lips scorching and hurt and a little triumphant. I gasped and Seb swept into me, thick and hot and full of passion.

Before I could put myself back together to react, he was gone, the door slamming behind him again. I touched a finger to my lips; they tingled, a little raw from the harshness of his beard rubbing against my skin. My heart was racing, the previous overtures of an ache settled in between my legs as a deep need.

Satiating that need would be a slippery slope, and I needed a different distraction, so I would do something other than touch myself and think about Seb. Exercise was normally the last thing I wanted to do after days on my feet with cramped fingers and a tired back, but *Themis* had a gym, and that sounded like a much better option.

SEVEN

WE HAD A FEW DAYS BEFORE OUR GUESTS ARRIVED, AND as a treat, Dom was running us at half staff for the next two nights. The staff who was off for the evening had free rein to go out and explore Tivat, while the rest of the crew stayed behind and worked as usual. I let Roy have the first night off, and I'd take the second night. Roy and Seb had elected to take the night off together, and I was looking forward to a boat without Seb. I wouldn't have to worry about watching him eat, running into him on the deck, or seeing him laugh and banter with the rest of the crew. After our kiss in my cabin that afternoon, he'd been all I could think about. I needed a break.

Cat was also staying on board that night, and we dedicated the early evening to going over the dinnerware and planning out the more formal dinners for the charter guests.

When we descended back down to the crew lounge, it was bustling with activity. Those going ashore were gathering, everyone dressed up for an evening out on the town.

I pulled out the prep work I'd done for the crew dinner and shooed a few people out of the galley. I set pots of water to boil, and within minutes I'd dropped the mussels in and the fresh briny aroma wafted around the galley.

"Hey, Marcella." Roy leaned against the counter.

Seb stepped up behind Roy. "Smells good." These were the first words Seb and I had exchanged since our kiss.

"Thank you." I refused to look at him. "It's a traditional Campanian dish, pasta with beans, garlic, white wine."

"*Pasta e fagioli con cozze*?" Roy asked.

I smiled at him. "Yes."

"Damn, I can't believe I'm missing this tonight," Roy said.

I kept a close eye on the pot, waiting for the mussels to open, while I pureed beans and diced parsley. Seb and Roy talked about their plans for some club and I tried not to listen, but they were in my galley and, while they tried to keep their voices down at first, their heckling and teasing each other made it impossible not to hear them.

"It's a shame we're not getting to Ibiza this year. You would love it, Seb. Lots of dancing and small bikinis. I could show you a thing or two on the dance floor there."

Seb scoffed. "You dance fine, for a white guy. Someday we'll go out in Miami."

"And you dance okay for a straight bloke."

There was a moment of silence and I focused harder on ignoring them . . . or at least looking like it. I peeked into the pot again and the mussels were starting to open, so I grabbed the tongs and a platter to pull them out.

The mussels I'd bought this morning were perfectly plump and juicy.

Out of the corner of my eye, I saw Seb placing a hand on Roy's shoulder. I could just barely hear him over the hiss of my pot. "It's fine, Roy."

Gio ducked his head in from the crew lounge and spotted Roy and Seb. "Guys, time to go."

Roy raised his voice. "See you tomorrow, Marce."

"Have fun, boys," I called out over my shoulder. I scooped out the last mussel and looked back. Seb caught my eye and held it, just for a moment, as he rounded the corner.

THE NEXT MORNING, I WAS UP BEFORE ROY, WHO WAS moving a little slower after his night out. I sat in the corner of the crew lounge, working on next week's provisioning order, when Roy came in to get started on breakfast. I was about to shout out a good morning when the door opened again and someone else came in.

"Sorry, man," Roy said.

"You apologize every morning, but I'm used to getting up with you now. It's good for me." Seb's voice still carried the gentle timbre of sleep. I couldn't see them, nor could they see me, since I was tucked into the corner of the booth.

I thought about saying something. I really did, but they started chatting before I could.

"Crazy night last night, eh, mate?"

Seb grunted.

"I'm surprised you didn't go home with one of those birds."

Birds? I hated the way Roy said it, slyly, like he was in on something. Of course two single guys would meet people last night. Maybe they even hooked up. Locals, single travelers . . . who were these birds?

After a moment's hesitation, Seb said, "They weren't my type."

Another pause.

"Shit, you make piss-poor coffee, man."

"I know, I know. But with all this British crew, you're the only coffee addict. You could go wake Marcella up and ask her to make that orgasm-inducing coffee for you."

"No, thanks." The words were sharp and bitter. When I first met Seb, he was the only one on *Odyssey* drinking espresso. One morning, I'd whipped him up an Italian coffee with *cremina,* sugar whipped with the first few drops of espresso from a moka pot. Seb had teared up in pleasure.

"Marcella's pretty," Roy said, and Seb snorted. The sound pierced my heart and made my hands clench in anger.

"For a woman . . . if you're into that," Roy continued.

"Marcella's not pretty," Seb stated. "She's gorgeous. And she makes better coffee than you." I heard him take a sip, and the quiet hung in the air. "I don't know what happened."

"Is there something you want to tell me about Marcella?" Roy probed.

Seb was silent. In the absence of their conversation, I could hear the snick of a blade cutting through something soft and moist; Roy was doing prep work.

Roy continued into Seb's silence. "Or can I just assume that one night you won't come back to our cabin, and I'll know where to find you if I need to?"

"It's not like that," Seb said. "She seems to hate me now."

Roy hummed in understanding.

"How's it going here, anyway?" Seb asked. "Do you like working for Marcella?"

A pang of guilt hit me. I shouldn't be listening in on conversations about me, especially when they crossed from personal to professional. But I couldn't bring myself to interrupt or leave. They'd both know I'd been here listening and intruding on a private conversation.

Fortunately, I was saved by a crackle on the radio. "Roy? Delivery's here."

"That's the fishmonger. Come help me?"

Seb and Roy both climbed the stairs out to the main deck and I was left alone again. Seb's words played over in my mind—*she seems to hate me now*—and I felt awful for making him feel this way. But hate was better than other feelings. It was less risky.

EIGHT

MY SANDALS CLICKED ON THE FLOOR AS I WALKED INTO the galley. Just like the previous night, the half of us off work for the evening were gathered in the lounge and galley, and chatter filled the air over the sounds of Roy cooking.

He spotted me and wolf-whistled. I grinned at him before taking a deep inhale of the Bolognese sauce that simmered on the stove, carefully holding back my long hair from the steam.

"Ready for your hot night out?" Roy asked.

"Cat and I are going to dinner." I tipped my chin at the more rambunctious crowd in the lounge. "Not to the club like the rest, but to a café."

He smiled and stirred. "Are you more of a quiet evening kind of girl?"

"Good food and good company. Yes, please."

"You look great." He eyed my pin-striped romper. "Don't you think so, Seb?" Roy's eyes snapped up over my shoulder, and I turned. Seb stood still in the doorway, eyes wandering along my body. My legs were on display—my favorite asset, and one hidden more often than not under chef's pants—and Seb's eyes devoured them.

In the heavy moment of silence, a memory surfaced of my legs pressed against Seb's torso, my ankles on either side of his neck and his eyes hot and intense on mine. It was the same look he was giving me now, and I could nearly see the scene echoed in his mind. My whole body tightened.

"Marcella?" Cat's voice broke the tension, and Roy cleared his throat next to me.

I pasted a smile on and pivoted toward Cat on the other side of the galley. Her olive-green wrap dress swayed as she leaned against the doorway. "Hey, yeah, I'm ready."

Passing Roy, I patted him on the back with my clutch. "Have a good service tonight."

"You got it."

I followed Cat, weaving through the rest of the crew, and we made our way up to the main deck. The sun had set already, but the sky was still colorful, lights flickering on in the city and in the sky. I felt a pang of longing for *Eik*—every evening, as often as we could, we'd watched the sunset together. Back in the professional world, I didn't have the luxury to stop meal prep for even a few minutes and appreciate the surroundings.

Cat stepped off the gangway with a sigh. "It's like flipping a switch from boss lady to regular human being."

"It certainly is," I agreed.

As we walked, Cat pointed out some sights around Tivat, and I asked her about activities in the area. Roy and I had traveled all over the city, but with work in mind. Cat, with her experiences here in the city and years of practice being a quick tourist, was full of advice for how to make the most of limited time.

She had picked out the café, and as we settled into the seats, she left her menu on the table and leaned close. "Did you bring the pictures?"

I pulled out my phone and she squealed. Together, we flipped through picture after picture from my time on *Eik*. Cat was fascinated, asking tons of questions in between ordering dinner and sipping our drinks. When I showed her a picture of the crew—me, Eivind, Jonas, Elayna, and Lila—on a hike in Tahiti, she grabbed my phone and squinted, carefully inspecting our faces.

"My God, these guys are young. And handsome. Holy crap." She fanned herself.

I pointed at the photo, naming each person.

"What a trip. Are you tired of talking about it?" she asked.

"No, not yet." I took the phone back, looking at the picture again. We'd been driving around Tahiti and stopped to watch the waves pound the cliffs and blast up through a blowhole. It was one of my last days with the crew. Lila squealed every time the waves crashed in, and Jonas and I, the oldest two, had rolled our eyes at the antics. I missed Jonas; we'd been close, him a steady rock holding the crew together. Eivind was the kind of guy who adored any food and was easy to please.

I shook off my nostalgia. It would be more work here, harder to please the charter guests and the Boyds, but it would be worth the reward.

Cat sipped her gin and tonic. "So, I hear you've worked with Seb before?"

"Yes," I said carefully. "In the Caribbean."

She folded her hands on the table in front of her. "I like working with him. He's mature for his age, I think." She watched me carefully. "When I came into the galley, it seemed like there was something going on?"

My whole body tensed. I was not going to be

causing drama on *Themis* and I certainly didn't want Cat to suspect anything was happening—because there wasn't. It was bad enough having Roy see our interactions together, and hearing the way he talked about me with Seb, I knew he had his suspicions.

"Nothing is going on with Seb," I said firmly. Maybe too firmly, based on the way one of Cat's eyebrows rose up. "What about you?"

"Me and Seb?" Cat's expression shifted to surprise and I quickly backtracked.

"No, I mean . . . you and anyone? Not Seb, obviously. Not that, like, he wouldn't be into you. I mean. He's . . . You're . . ."

She smirked at my stammering.

"There's a guy from another boat who I hook up with occasionally, when we're in port together. And one guy in Barcelona I can call up sometimes." She shrugged. "But nothing serious."

I changed the topic to ask her about Barcelona—a port we'd be visiting by the end of the season—and she moved on too, thankfully. I didn't want to think about Seb hooking up with anyone, didn't want to think about how he had hooked up with me while we worked together, so what would keep him from hooking up with another coworker?

———

It was the first day of the charter, six a.m., and *Themis* was a flutter of activity already. The guests were scheduled to arrive at nine, and we expected to leave the dock at ten to set sail. Activity on the deck above me had me hustling to move faster and get out of the cabin. I twisted my long dark hair into my usual bun, threw on chef pants and a *Themis* tee, and went out the door.

I slid open the doors to the master suite, the last time I'd get to take the shortcut through it until the guests left. The room was spotless, linens intricately folded, bar cart sparkling in the corner, and the shades thrown open.

I passed through the atrium and guest cabins before arriving into the galley. It was quiet, though I knew people were up.

After slipping on my apron and chef jacket, I affixed the radio to my belt and slid the earpiece in. "Morning, all."

The radio crackled before Dom came in. "Morning, Marcella. Flight check shows on-time delivery."

"Excellent, thanks. Catarina, you on?"

Instead of answering, the door opened in the main deck lounge and Cat's dainty steps echoed down the stairs. She smiled at me before speaking into the radio. "Cat here, I'm in the galley. We'll get cracking." She had her clipboard ready to go for notes and set hers down next to mine.

"Morning, Cat."

"Good morning. I started the coffee maker upstairs. Would you like a cup?"

I grimaced at the idea of the instant grounds Cat liked. I tilted my head toward the espresso machine. "No, thanks, I'll get this thing started."

She nodded. We went over our notes together, refreshing our memories and confirming the schedule. Continental breakfast would be served when the guests arrived, and we would depart at ten.

Crew filtered in and out while we talked, grabbing supplies, firing up machines, getting the day started, everyone knowing where they needed to be. Cat excused herself, and joined her crew while I started in on baking.

Voices came down from upstairs, Roy's and Seb's, and two sets of footsteps followed.

Seb paused when he saw me.

"Hey, mate. Warn a bloke if you've got brakes on. I nearly spilled my tea."

Seb stepped aside and Roy gave me a cheeky grin. "You got the espresso machine going early this morning, yeah? A little extra boost for those of us who were up too late last night."

"I wasn't up too late last night," Seb muttered. "I was doing my job."

The night before clients arrived, the exterior crew started their night watches in preparation for a week of being on anchor. When the boat was out at anchor, someone was always on watch. Seb had had the graveyard shift last night, but still had to be up to care for the guests and help his team out. We all had our own version of twenty-hour workdays during a charter.

"Right, squeegeeing windows and writing the same numbers down eleventy billion times." Roy started rummaging around the fridges and pulling fruit out. "At least Marce and I get 'normal' hours."

I tried to ignore Roy and Seb chattering away. I knew it wouldn't last long, since Seb probably had only a fifteen-minute break. I focused my attention on laminating my croissant dough. Roll, fold, turn, roll, fold, turn.

"Oi, mate, stop eating all my hard work."

"Stop making fun of my job."

"I gotta do it now before you become the boss of all of us." Roy saluted Seb. "Captain Alvarez."

"Don't get your panties in a twist. We've got a few years."

"Right, well, I'm still crossing my fingers for you on the regatta deal."

"What's the regatta deal?" I asked, curiosity getting the better of me.

Seb leaned back against the counter and finished chewing. "It's a training program at the regatta. Basically, I'd be taking a day or two off to get some sailing coaching in. Consider it job training."

"You want to be a sailor?"

Seb shrugged. "I may not be as passionate about it as some people, but having some skills in place and some knowledge around racing would help my career prospects."

"Sailing's actually pretty great. I think you would like it."

"You know," Roy said thoughtfully, "*Themis* has a little sailing dinghy. We should take it out next time we get an off day. I bet Clarissa could teach us a thing or two."

Seb looked at me, tilting his head and narrowing his eyes. "Why bother Clarissa? I bet Marce could show us how to sail the tender."

"I bet I could," I fired back.

"Yeah, so which part of the sailboat was intriguing to you? Was it the wind in your hair or the sound of the boat cutting through the waves? Or was it the captain?" Seb bit out.

"Excuse me?" I set my measuring cup down

forcefully. "What exactly does that have to do with anything?"

"I'm just wondering which part of sailing off with two strange men attracted your attention."

"Seb." Roy laughed nervously. "I've got a knife—don't make me stab you. Leave my boss alone."

I crossed my arms and fully faced Seb, glaring at him.

"It's an honest question," he said, eyebrows pinching together and anger flushing his cheeks.

"I do *not* regret my time on *Eik* and how dare you insinuate anything. Have you been to Panama, the Marquesas, Tahiti?"

"Well," Seb drawled, full of sarcasm, "I'm glad you got around."

I sucked in a breath and so did Roy. Even if Seb had been hurt, that was no excuse for him to be so cruel. I was hurt too, and I'd lost more than he had.

"Mate, too far."

"What the hell is the matter with you? We've got a big day and don't need your negativity around here. Fuck off." I leaned forward, angry enough to physically push him out of my kitchen if I had to.

Seb slammed his cup down. "Fine, I will fuck off." He turned for the stairs, flashing two fingers at Roy. "Later, man."

I huffed a breath and turned back to my dough, my fingers shaky.

"Marce—" Roy began, but I cut him off.

"Don't. It's fine." I wiped my hands on my apron, shaking them out, attempting to bring the atmosphere back to normal.

Roy eyed me carefully, but picked up his knife and started slicing fruit. The tension in the galley was heavy, and I tried to relax and roll my shoulders, blinking away tears of frustration. I had a job to do.

NINE

I THREW MYSELF INTO MY WORK. THIS FIRST presentation was an easy one, and relied on freshness and quality. The stews helped us take everything upstairs.

Bok, one of the stews, a petite Korean-born Brit, was doing some last-minute polishing of the silverware. She smiled and greeted us. Clarissa wavered nearby, absentmindedly tidying the service station. Unlike most of the crew, Clarissa was designated for two jobs as a deck stew. While we had no guests, she was part of the exterior team, working with the deckhands. When we did have guests, she worked on the stew side. She fidgeted with her uniform, looking less comfortable in the formal uniform the stews wore, a modest navy dress, than she did in the casual deck uniform.

"Want to go over the menu really quick?"

They both nodded, and I pointed out each dish as I walked around the table, the two of them following.

When I finished, I turned back to Roy. "Anything look amiss to you?"

"No, ma'am."

"All right then." I checked my watch and sent Roy a grin. "At ease, soldier."

He laughed and we had a few minutes to relax. Roy leaned against the bar and chatted with Will. I stepped to the starboard side of the boat and looked out over the marina. Stacked up along piers were rows and rows of smaller boats: sail and power. Beyond that, Tivat's waterfront held gleaming white concrete and thick palm trees. The terra-cotta roofs were bright against the blue sky. I'd seen enough of the nearby area to know that this was one of the swankier parts of Tivat, and I'd heard from the other crew members about the marina amenities, like infinity pools and saunas.

Seb came around a corner and met my eye. A look I couldn't read passed over his face, and I glared at him. He glanced around, then walked toward me.

"Look, Marcella . . ."

I raised an eyebrow, incredulous. "Seriously? Not now."

"I just wanted to apologize. I went too far this morning."

"Yes, you did. Stay out of my galley." I looked back out at the city, trying to pin the details of Tivat in my mind.

"Marce, I really am sorry. You're just confusing."

I ignored him.

"Hey, I'm trying to apologize here. Obviously, I was hurt from our night in Antigua and it didn't mean anything to you—"

"The van's here," I interrupted. "And you don't know anything about what matters to me, otherwise you wouldn't be picking a fight with me right before my first charter. I need to focus." It had meant something to me, but what was the point of admitting that? We needed to let this blow over to be civil around each other.

"No distractions, right?"

I nodded. "No distractions."

He watched me for a moment. Car doors slammed and shouts from kids echoed off the water.

"Okay. I know this is important. That's not— I wasn't trying—" Seb pinched the bridge of his nose and took a deep breath. "We can do this, Marce. No distractions."

"Good." I nodded stiffly and then left Seb behind, joining the rest of the service crew.

The mood shifted on board as the guests climbed up to the lazarette of *Themis,* the staff turning on practiced smiles and straightening up.

The waiting deckhands clamored to the van to open doors and assist our guests in getting on board. *Themis* was docked starboard-side-to, and the narrow gangway was extended out to the dock.

The stews waited at the top of the ramp and then took over, giving a brief tour of the deck area and taking drink orders. With nineteen crew aboard for ten guests, there were plenty of hands to help out.

Roy and I stood by the beverage station, letting the rest of the team take the lead. Dom introduced himself, glad-handing the adults. We had two couples and a nanny on board, in addition to five kids.

Between the ages of seven and twelve, according to our dossiers, the children boarded the boat and immediately took off running down the deck. There were squeals and crashes as they left a destructive wake behind them.

Neither the parents nor the nanny did anything to control the kids.

"Hello! Who would like to see the game room?" Clarissa called out.

Five pairs of eyes snapped to her, followed by shouts of excitement, and Percy opened the door.

With the guests now on board, the real work began.

I HAD ALWAYS BEEN LOOKING FOR A JOB THAT WOULD take me to unique and exotic destinations. The irony of having that adventurous job was that, sometimes, I would see the scenery only through the window of the galley. And most of the time, I wouldn't look up at all.

Dom had taken us off the dock right on time. Finally I felt *Themis* move underneath my feet, and instead of looking out over the neighborhoods of Tivat, the scenery shifted. I knew our schedule, but little else. Sometime later, we anchored out in the Bay of Kotor—the view from the window was calm water and cloud-capped mountains off in the distance.

In the darkness while we prepped dinner, *Themis* crossed from Montenegro to Croatia, but we were too busy to notice. Our guests had elected to have a three-course meal on their first night, in addition to starting dining at ten o'clock. It was nearly one a.m. by the time I pushed the last dessert plate out the door.

I waited five minutes, cleaning myself up, before climbing the stairs to greet our guests.

The foursome was loud and I could hear them from the base of the stairs. A brief vertigo hit me when I reached the main deck and saw the lights of the coast passing by. *Themis* was stable enough that I nearly forgot that we were on the move until I glanced out the window. We were probably approaching Dubrovnik, our destination for the night.

"*Buona sera*. Mr. and Mrs. Delmonico, Mr. and Mrs. Granger, how was your meal this evening?"

While the men were dressed more casually, the women sported full makeup, manicured nails, and reedy bodies. Perfume masked any of the aromas of my hard work—even the fresh baked bread, which had filled the galley with a mouthwatering yeasty scent, was overpowered.

"Chef Baresi," Mr. Delmonico greeted me, and offered me a handshake. "Everything was wonderful. That veal dish was a big hit with us."

"I'm so glad you enjoyed it. Are there any changes you'd like to see to the general menu?"

"No, everything was—"

"Dear," Mrs. Granger interrupted, not meeting my eye. "Lighter lunches please. Salads—the pastas were far too heavy."

"Yes, ma'am. Anything else?"

"Some fish for tomorrow night's dinner. And can

we do the sit-down again? This was lovely." She delicately placed her napkin over her barely touched plate.

The schedule for tomorrow had been for a family-style, more casual dinner, but that didn't matter. "Certainly."

"Good, good. That will be all, thank you." I was dismissed.

"Yes, ma'am, please enjoy the rest of your evening."

In the galley I quickly jotted down some notes for tomorrow, going over the day and trying to pinpoint what I could improve upon. Roy had finished a majority of the dishes during the main course, and I'd sent him off to bed, leaving me alone to think. In this industry, there were always people who treated you a little less. That was the feeling I got from Mrs. Granger, and I would do my best to make sure she had nothing to complain about.

The door leading to the crew quarters opened up and I called out without looking up. "I thought I told you to get to bed."

"Well, aren't we demanding?" came Seb's voice in response. "Who exactly is getting in your bed now?"

I shot a glare at him. "I thought you were Roy."

He yawned and stretched. "Good luck with that."

"Seb, knock it off. I'm tired and at the end of my day."

He had the decency to look contrite. "Sorry."

I returned to my papers. "What are you doing down here anyway?"

"I was just getting up from my nap and starting my night shift. Are they still up?"

"Yes. And still going."

Seb leaned his elbows on the counter across from me. "How did dinner go?"

I looked up at him, surprised he was moving on from our anger and interested. "Okay, I think. A few adjustments to make, and they barely touched their desserts. I'm not happy about that."

"What did you serve them?"

"Tiramisu."

Seb's lips quivered. "Not panna cotta?"

"Ha. No."

One time on *Odyssey* I had made panna cotta and given Seb a taste. I described it like flan, but unbeknownst to me, Seb's experience with flan was the Cuban dessert his *abuela* had made, with sweetened condensed milk and evaporated milk instead of cream. The flan Seb grew up with was very different from the panna cotta I was raised on, much sweeter and thicker.

Seb had a serious sweet tooth.

"I have a tiramisu left in the fridge. Want to try it?"

It was an olive branch, of sorts. If he could try to move on, so could I. Seb studied me and slowly grinned.

"*Sí*, that would be good."

"You'll have a sugar high for your watch," I warned. I pulled open the fridge and handed Seb the delicate glass bowl that housed the tiramisu.

"Better a sugar high than asleep on the job."

I crossed my arms and leaned back against the cool of the stainless steel. Seb eagerly pulled a spoon out of the flatware drawer and scooped up some of the delicate dessert, ensuring he got a combination of the ladyfingers and cream.

The spoon slipped into his mouth, and I watched his lips slide off the metal. Seb's facial hair usually edged on the border of scruff and beard, but today it was longer, fuller.

He closed his eyes and I flashed back to that night, his eyes closed in a different kind of pleasure, dirty words coming out of his lips. I remembered a groan, or did I hear it now? I refocused my eyes on Seb. He was watching me, swallowing the bite, spoon poised over the bowl.

"Do you want some?" Was his voice a little bit

more gravelly than normal? Seb's tongue flicked out, licking a tiny bit of cream off his bottom lip.

I knew the tiramisu was good—I'd tasted it along each step of the way and I'd made this dish from scratch so many times, I could make it by heart. But I wondered, what would Seb do if I said yes?

I nodded, and Seb plunged the spoon back down and scraped a bite out for me. He took a step toward me, holding up the spoon. His eyes were focused on my mouth, dark and intent, and I realized there were far too many thoughts in my head about spooning tiramisu in indecent places and licking it off. Seb stood waiting—it was too late to back out, even if I wanted to.

Stepping forward, I leaned in toward the spoon. Seb watched my lips, his expression growing cocky and sure. I was about to close my mouth around the spoon when he pulled it back, and I clicked my mouth closed on air.

"Seb!" I flushed red and aimed a light punch at his stomach. He laughed, but chased after me when I backed off.

My back hit the cooler, Seb's front pressed up against me, the hardness of his body molding me to him. His elbow met the stainless steel behind me, holding the bowl up above our heads. My heart raced, and Seb's breath matched my own: shallow and quick, disturbing the wisps of hair around my ear.

He was too close; we looked at each other for a moment before his eyes dropped to my mouth.

The spoon hovered and dipped toward me. I opened my mouth and let him slide the spoon in, swallowing and sucking on it.

Seb's breathing became ragged. His forehead thunked against the cooler door and he let the spoon out of my mouth slowly, sliding it against my bottom lip.

The door at the top of the stairs opened, and the laughter and recklessness from upstairs flooded down. When the door slammed shut, blocking off most of the noise, I could hear footsteps coming down the stairs and my eyes widened.

"Seb," I whispered. He didn't budge. "Seb!" I called more urgently and pressed my hand against his chest, shoving him back a step. He blinked at me.

I bent over the paperwork again just as Toby, one of the deckhands, rounded the corner.

"Hey, man, ya gonna take over for me? I'm bushed and they're still partying like hell up there."

Seb mumbled around another bite of tiramisu and I gathered my papers up. I cleared my throat, attempting to shake off the spell. It was too easy to remember the Seb who had been more than a coworker, but also a friend—and, for one night, a lover.

"Gentlemen, good night. See you in the morning."

I rushed out, quickly forcing myself to relegate Seb back into the proper box—or risk my job again.

TEN

BETWEEN A LATE NIGHT SHIFTING THE MENU, TOSSING and turning over memories of Seb, and being up early to handle breakfast orders, I was running on minimal sleep. The crew food was out, and I made the special dishes for our guests. Roy was assisting, chopping and dicing as my sous chef.

Harper, one of the deckhands, flounced into the galley, seething. "One of the lounge chairs upstairs is completely ruined. That bratty girl Elsa," Harper spit. "She got ahold of some markers and 'decorated' one of the white lounge chairs up on the bridge deck, the ones right off the bedroom where her parents were! How can they be so negligent? Where is the nanny?"

Roy and I exchanged glances at her tirade but had to keep working. There was nothing we could say anyway. Harper knew what to do: the lounge chair had to disappear and we'd deal with it in port once our charter week was done.

Hours later Clarissa was upset and moaning to Bok. "Can you believe they asked Dom to take down the sails? What is the point of chartering this boat if you don't want to actually sail her?"

No one answered, but the answer hung over our heads: they could afford whatever they wanted, and if they wanted the most unique, luxurious statement, they hired *Themis*.

We got back to work, and *Themis* cruised off the coast of Croatia while I multitasked like crazy. Bread was baking, pastries were being stuffed, and a red pepper coulis simmered on the stove. I took a deep breath, pausing the first time since the breakfast rush had started.

A throat cleared; Bok stood behind me, wringing her hands. "Marcella, I think we have a problem."

"Roy, can you keep an eye on this coulis?" I tilted my head for Bok to follow me to the sink so I could wash my hands. "What's wrong?"

"Mrs. Granger wants another smoothie, but she said the one from yesterday was not the smoothie she ordered. She said it didn't have spirulina in it, and the ratios were completely wrong for the request she sent in."

I shook my head. "What request? She sent in no request. *Merda.*"

Walking over to the cupboard, I pulled out my portfolio and flipped through my notes to her preference sheet. Bok leaned in, reading over my shoulder.

"What's spirulina?" she asked.

"An algae powder. And something I definitely do not have on board." I sighed and closed my eyes. "Nor is it something I'll be able to find soon. Maybe I could have found it in Split, but we've already left."

I flipped over to our itinerary. We were due in Hvar tonight, a resort island off the coast. I closed my eyes and took a deep breath. "Okay, we have two issues here: one, I don't have the recipe for her smoothie; and two, we don't have spirulina. I'm going to go upstairs and talk to Mrs. Granger. If there are more ingredients we need to get, then it would be better not to have to make two shopping trips."

Talking to Mrs. Granger took all of my best patience. The woman was lounging on the aft sundeck, drinking her way through Will's painkillers. He nodded at me from the bar, and by the look on his face, I guessed the drinks were being watered down already.

"Chef Trey was supposed to email you the recipe. I have one every day," she said. Despite that, she couldn't tell me any of the other ingredients beyond "some whey powder" and agave syrup.

Back downstairs, Roy was still working in the galley, chatting with Seb, who was in for a snack. Bok and Cat were in the lounge, leaning over laptops and papers. Cat looked up. "Any luck?"

"Not really. She doesn't know much, but I've got the number for her personal chef."

"We've been searching for spirulina in Hvar but no luck. There are some health food stores in Split that might carry it." Cat tilted the laptop my way and I could see the map results.

"How far is Split?"

Cat winced. "An hour and a half by ferry."

"Merda. Let me call my provisioning company and see if they can run something over."

"I have a few contacts on Hvar—let me see if any of them have a faster option." Cat pulled out her phone and started tapping.

Out of the corner of my eye, I saw Seb rinse his dishes out in the sink and give Roy a fist bump. "Later." And he was out the door.

My calls were fruitless. Our schedule would get thrown off if we waited too long in Hvar, and I couldn't allow that to happen. Cat hadn't been very successful either. Getting ahold of people in the hospitality industry in peak season was hard.

Good news came in the call with the personal chef. Not only did he give me the recipe, while making sure I knew it hadn't been his fault that I didn't have it, but he also gave me some advice for Mrs. Granger's usual menu. There were several tips he mentioned that hadn't been indicated at all on the preference sheet.

The door opened and Seb strolled in. "You're looking for spirulina, right?"

"Yes."

"I've got some." He held up his phone. "A buddy of mine is working on a yacht that's already anchored in Hvar, and they've got spirulina on board." He turned his phone toward me to show me a picture. "This is the right stuff, yeah?"

"What, really?" I stood up and grabbed his phone. "Oh my God. You are amazing!"

Seb grinned at me, all cocky and pleased.

"How did you manage this?"

"I went up to the pilothouse and Dom helped me check the names of the boats in the area in the identification system. We recognized a few of them that employed yachties who either of us knew from other ports, and we made some calls on the radio."

"That's bloody brilliant, mate. Good job," Roy called from the galley.

"Yeah, wow." That was clever, and something I

wouldn't have thought to do. Seb had taken a risk, called in favors for me, and rescued me in a minor crisis. This was the Seb I'd known before we'd crossed a line: helpful and supportive.

Cat scooted out of the booth and high-fived Seb on her way out. "Nice teamwork, Seb."

"Running down to the walk-in," Roy called out over his shoulder as he strode out the door.

That left just me and Seb in the crew lounge.

"I better get back to lunch."

"Yeah, I've got work to get to as well." Seb rubbed the back of his neck.

"Listen, thanks for the help today. That was creative thinking and . . . I appreciate it."

He nodded, but hesitated before pulling the door open and heading upstairs.

Four hours later I had a bottle of spirulina in my galley. I immediately blended the smoothie per the instructions, and Bok took it upstairs to Mrs. Granger, who had just returned from a Jet Ski trip.

I took a long spoon and scooped up some of the remnants at the bottom of the blender to taste it and I grimaced. Bland and slightly bitter.

Bok returned a few minutes later with the smoothie still in hand. She set the glass carefully down on the counter. "Mrs. Granger has changed her mind about the smoothie."

I sighed and closed my eyes. Behind me, Roy groaned, and I heard his forehead hit the counter repeatedly.

All the work we'd put in trying to please our client, just thrown away. Some people had no class.

ELEVEN

Day four of the charter and I didn't know where we were. Somewhere in Croatia still, but the view out the window was much the same.

Roy and I were plating up lunch service for the guests. Crew lunch was out on trays on the galley island and the kitchen was loud with staff.

Most guests willing to spend hundreds of thousands of dollars on a weeklong vacation saw us only as demure, nearly silent genies who granted their every wish. But in reality, once we stepped away and into the crew quarters, we were anything but quiet. The conversation always centered around the galley and mealtime; thus, I knew everything.

Since we were underway so often, Dom was up at the bridge deck most of the time. He was fairly isolated, working with the exterior crew to satisfy the guests, but also putting on a show *for* the guests.

I rarely interacted with the guests compared with the stews. But I could tell how things were going based on the talk around the table, and it was not going well.

After the lounge chair incident, the kids had continued to run around unsupervised. They'd somehow all worked together to sneak buckets of sand back to the boat, and dumped all the sand in one of the guest cabins to "build sandcastles." One of our television remotes was missing—Cat suspected it had gone overboard.

The adults weren't much better. They'd purposefully given our crew the slip while in port one evening and the whole schedule had been fucked. I'd had to hold dinner for a few hours and we'd missed our departure time for the next stop. Mrs. Delmonico had vomited in her cabin the third morning and neglected to mention it. All three women had complained about the food, picking at their meals and then sending orders down for diet smoothies.

The whiteboard had a new quote on it: *"The only time to eat diet food is while you're waiting for the steak to cook." —Julia Child*

We were frayed. Guests rarely acted like this. The ultrarich who rented the yachts I'd worked on were demanding, specific, and detail oriented, but never malicious.

It came to a head that fourth evening. We were anchored for the night, and dinner service was over early, thank God. Roy and I were finishing cleaning up and he'd be heading off to bed soon, and I had settled in to finish the menu for tomorrow. The day had run us both particularly ragged, with the guests on board the whole time, requesting snacks and cocktails all day. I jumped when the door to the crew cabins flew open, slamming against the wall, and Seb stormed in.

"Call Dom," he told me tersely.

I clicked on my radio and told Dom to get down to the galley for a crew situation. When he arrived, Seb pulled him aside and tried to lower his voice, but his frustration carried in the small, empty space. I caught words like *naked* and *grabbing*.

Dom pinched the bridge of his nose, something I'd watched him do far too often this week. He checked his watch, and took off for the crew quarters, hailing Gio on the radio. Seb paced the length of the galley, turned, and paced back. His jaw was tense, his annoyance seeping through every pore.

Roy's wide eyes connected with mine, confusion drawing his eyebrows together. "Everything okay, mate?"

"There's a fucking naked nanny in my bed, so no, everything is not okay." Seb stomped through to the lounge but was back moments later.

"Oh bugger."

Roy's Britishism made Seb chuckle darkly. "This is by far the worst charter I've ever done. Where the fuck do they find these nut jobs?"

"Having enough bloody money doesn't give you human decency, that's for sure."

Seb sighed. "I have to be up in three hours to start my night watch. I didn't get a nap in today because we had to refuel the Jet Ski since they've used it so much. And now there's a drunk-off-her-ass woman who won't leave me alone."

"She just showed up in your bed?" I asked.

"I was asleep, and she came into my room, stripped down, and crawled into bed with me. I thought . . ."

Seb's face flushed and he averted his eyes. He spun around and paced the floor again. "I thought something else was happening, and as soon as I realized it, I pushed her away. Yeah, she'd been a little handsy before, but I *did not* encourage it." He looked me in the eye. "I swear, Marce."

I glanced at Roy. "I don't care, Seb." My stomach rolled at the lie. I did care. Indignance for Seb made me angry, but even worse was the thought that he *could* have slept with her. I had no claim. "It's not my business," I reminded him—and myself.

He just grunted and swung back around. "I need sleep."

I tried to focus back on my paperwork while Roy worked to lighten Seb's mood.

The door opened again and Gio and Dom came through. "She's gone, Seb. We put her back in her room for the night. I know we don't normally lock cabin doors around here, but make sure you lock yours behind you from now on. In fact, that needs to be the policy for everyone for the rest of this trip. And, unfortunately, she, um, made a mess of herself in your bed."

Poor Seb just could not catch a break.

"Fuck it, I'm sleeping in the lounge."

Dom grimaced. "Sorry, man. I wish we had a spare bed for you, but I don't want to risk putting you upstairs. I did call Bok down, though, and she helped me strip your bed. But the mattress should probably dry out a bit."

Seb's face fell. "Can I quit?"

Dom slapped him on the back. "We'll get the steamer out tomorrow and really clean it for you. But no, you can't leave me over some stupid shit a client does. You'll have a good story and we all owe you some beers after this. I don't suppose you want to bunk with me? The bed's not big but we can cuddle real close."

Knocking Dom's arm off him, Seb conceded a half smile to the joke and lumbered off to the lounge with a half-hearted wave over his shoulder. "You bastard. Night then."

Dom and Gio left, and Roy and I exchanged a few glances while we tried to clean as quietly as we could.

Despite our attempts, the doors still clamored open and closed a few times with staff coming and going. I wished Roy a good night, and watched him leave for the crew quarters.

Seb tossed on the bench as I gathered my things. I hesitated at the door. "Seb?"

He grunted and twisted over to look at me. "Marce?" His voice was hoarse and tired.

I bit my lip. My heartstrings tugged for Seb, just trying to get by the best he could when the job could be shit sometimes. This was dumb—and risky—and I knew it. But that didn't stop me. "Do you want to come sleep in my cabin?"

"Marce . . ." His voice was softened by my kindness. He studied me, and I fidgeted under his inspection. "Yeah, okay."

Wordlessly, he followed me through the boat, up and over the main deck to my cabin. Mercifully, the deck was empty save Will, who was cleaning up the bar. He looked up and nodded at us, but kept his focus on his task.

In the cabin, I set my stuff down on my little desk and retreated to the head to prepare for bed and give Seb some privacy. I was too tired for much, but I brushed my teeth and washed my face. By the time I reentered the room, Seb was asleep facedown on my bed. He'd stripped to his boxers, and for the first time since I'd joined *Themis,* I could really stare at him without being caught.

Ever since we'd met, he'd always seemed to feel when my eyes were on him. I was always caught staring, and in the beginning, on *Odyssey,* I'd been given a cocky smirk. Since coming to *Themis,* though, it had been hurt and anger.

I watched him for a minute in the dim lighting, seeing Seb in a soft way I'd never noticed before. Selfishly, I wanted him here, to protect him, even though he wasn't mine.

Then it occurred to me that I needed to fit on the bed too. Seb would be up in a few hours, so I should give him the outside of the bed, but that meant I needed to get to the inside.

Carefully, I placed my palm on the mattress on the other side of Seb and swung a leg over his body. I shifted my weight, straddling him and trying not to touch or jostle. I held my breath and leaned down, sliding onto my side of the bed.

Seb shifted and I froze. His voice was muffled by the pillow, sleepy and confused. "Marce, that you this time?"

I gently touched his back, and the muscles flexed as Seb shifted next to me. "Yeah, it's me," I whispered.

He exhaled a big breath and reached out, sliding a hand across my stomach. Immediately his body relaxed, his breathing evening out. I sighed and reached up to turn off the reading light. Lying still in the dark, I felt the bed gently moving with each inhale and exhale. Fingers twitched lightly against my stomach. I ran my fingers through his, stilling the movement, and closed my eyes.

It would be so comfortable, so easy, to let him in again. But how could I keep myself from getting burned?

TWELVE

OUR GUESTS WERE GONE, FINALLY GONE. *THEMIS* WAS A ghost town, as Dom gave us all two days off: one to catch up on sleep and one to enjoy a day in Split. The staff was told to help themselves to anything they wanted in the galley, as long as they cleaned up afterward.

The second day, I slept in as much as I could before dressing in some comfortable shoes and stepping off the boat. We had tied up to the wharf in Split, called the West Bank, which had a long promenade for pedestrians. I followed the pavement until it dead-ended, and then I crossed over and into the city.

Yacht crew had limited time in port, so we'd perfected how to get as much done as possible in one day. Others might be off renting cars or scooters and maximizing their distance. I was more about maximizing the effort, and was going to see as much by foot as I could.

I climbed the Marjan Hill Stairs up to the observation deck, a meager part of the entire hill, but enough to get me a view over the harbor. *Themis,* with her unique rigging, drew the eye, but there were other yachts here too, and cruise ships across the bay. This reminded me of a hike I'd done with Seb in Antigua. I half expected to see him today, stretching his legs and finding the best view.

The morning after the nanny incident—as the staff was all calling it—I had woken up to an empty bed. Seb had slipped out in the early hours, but his scent was still on my sheets. I had rolled over and pressed my face into the linen, taking a big inhale before rolling off and getting up.

I had barely seen Seb since then. He would pop in for a quick bite to eat, but he didn't linger with Roy. My sous chef had gone quiet too. I didn't know what to make of it, but my own feelings for Seb were confusing enough.

Climbing back down, I crossed into the city center, walking through cobbled streets tightly lined with old buildings with terra-cotta roofs. Street names—any words, really—were written in a language that felt clunky on my tongue and had diacritical marks that baffled me. I walked the Riva, a pedestrian path in the city center waterfront in view of the Venetian Tower, and zigzagged through to temples and cathedrals. When I was tired, I sat at a café and ordered local pastries—*fritule* and *kroštule*—before getting up again to walk it all off.

I rarely shopped, but as I passed a window display, a moka pot caught my eye. Seb's sweet tooth extended to coffee, and one night—the one that popped up into my thoughts way too often—I had made Seb an espresso with cremina just like I drank at home. It was like the *cafecito* Seb drank back in his neighborhood in Miami. I had watched while Seb sipped that coffee, sweetened with sugar and the first drops of the moka, and his eyes had closed in pleasure.

"This is the best coffee I've ever had," he had said.

And then he'd kissed me.

This moka pot in the window of a tiny shop had brought a rush of memories—and sparked an idea. I knew just how to repay Seb for his favor.

With my purchase in hand, I made my way back to the galley of *Themis* and pulled my sous chef aside.

"First you boil some water," I instructed Roy.

He tossed a look at me and I smirked. *Oh, just wait.*

"Then you fill the base of the moka pot with the hot water. Take the freshly ground beans and put them in the filter. Tap it a few times." I demonstrated by tapping the metal container on the counter. "This goes in here; the top gets screwed back on. Then set it to boil again."

"Okay, so we're boiling the water, putting it in a fancy pot, and boiling it again. Just to be clear," Roy teased.

"I've seen you make tea. If you got any more particular about how you make it, I bet you would be qualified to serve the queen."

"Fair 'nough."

"Okay, this is the part you really have to watch." I flipped the lid of the top open and Roy and I peered in. "See how it's forming some liquid? That's the steam rising up through the coffee."

"Huh. Fancy."

"Now, with this here, the first coffee, we take this glass with a bit of sugar in it and pour the first coffee in."

"Like the first press of olives."

"Exactly. Set the rest back to finish boiling and while the first few drips are still fresh, we whip the sugar mixture." I whipped the spoon furiously around the glass until the first coffee became foamy and whipped. "This is called the cremina. Then we pour a mug of the final brew, spoon some of the cremina in, and enjoy."

Roy looked at the coffee skeptically. "You know I'm not a coffee drinker."

"But you are a good chef," I said. "And every chef knows to taste the food and judge the flavor before they serve it."

Roy took a sip and blanched. "Ugh, so bitter." He handed the mug back to me. "I'll pass, thanks."

"But can you make it now? We have the pot; someone might want a cup of the good stuff."

"Yes, I can make your special coffee now. Jeez. Don't you have work to be doing? Shoo, I've got to prepare dinner."

I took a sip and closed my eyes. So. Good.

"Here." Roy thrust my portfolio into my hands. "Go upstairs, enjoy the gorgeous day, and do some menu planning."

AFTER TWO DAYS OFF, I HAD SOME TIME AND ENERGY TO spare before our first morning management meeting after the charter. I sat outside at the bar and sipped my coffee, relishing the first time in months with a real *caffè*. Justin and I had been corresponding via email to get some of the basic plans sketched out for his and Natasha's upcoming visit and I had a few notes jotted down for ideas. My eyes darted between the paperwork and the Split skyline, memories of walking through the town yesterday warming my heart.

I had a few days to prepare for the Boyds' arrival. We'd spend a long weekend together, and I had two objectives: I had to wow Justin and Natasha with their meals during their stay, and we were going to do a menu tasting for the regatta.

The regatta was a two-day event, and *Themis* would be departing in the morning and spending the entire day out at sea as a spectator boat. We'd have fifty people on board, and I'd be serving a buffet lunch and snacks throughout the day.

The last night would be the awards ceremony, with a celebratory party afterward on *Themis* for a hundred people. Justin and I planned for displays and passed canapés. Additional staff would be brought in to help with prep, service, and clean up, but the responsibility sat with me—I would do most of the cooking and presentation myself, with Roy helping me.

"Hey, Marcella." Dom sat on the stool next to me. "What did you get up to yesterday?"

"Walked around town, enjoying the sights. Split has some beautiful history. What did you do?"

"Called my kids, mostly. We're trying to work out a way for me to see them before we sail to the Caribbean this year."

In November, the busy season ended in the Mediterranean. The temperatures cooled and the weather got a bit less predictable, so many boats would head across the Atlantic to the Caribbean for the high season there.

Gio and Cat came out of the crew stairs with their morning beverages and Edie joined us from the bow. Dom and I shifted to the table and the meeting got started.

"The good news is that our guests are gone."

A small chorus of cheers went up.

"Now, the bad news is, I haven't gotten word from the broker yet about tipping. It doesn't mean we haven't been tipped," Dom rushed to add, seeing our crestfallen faces. "It's just that we haven't gotten anything yet."

I'd heard stories of nightmare guests not tipping, but it had never actually happened to me. As the head chef, I got paid extremely well, and then you factor in tips and almost no living expenses, and I was doing just fine. But much of our younger, less experienced crew was still working their way up the ladder and the tips could sometimes surpass their actual paycheck.

"But I will let you know as soon as I hear anything," Dom continued. "I do want you to know that this was a particularly tough charter, maybe the worst I've ever seen." He tilted his head. "Except for that time someone brought a live cow onto the boat, but yeah. Everyone did exceptionally well given the situation. Thank you for your hard work, and be sure your staff recuperates as needed. In the meantime, let's talk about this week."

In two days, we would leave for Corfu, where Natasha and Justin would meet us. It was a five-hundred-kilometer trip along the Adriatic Coast, and we would do it all in one go. Then we had a few days to prepare in Corfu for our owners. Upon their arrival, we'd spend three days circumnavigating the island.

"We'll have an all-staff meeting the day before the Boyds arrive. Undoubtedly, Natasha and Justin will have some modifications or projects they want to make to the boat before the regatta, so we'll meet again after and tackle those before we leave for Malta."

We went on to discuss projects that needed to be addressed, repercussions from the charter. Cat was up to her eyeballs in cleaning, and was going to have to bring in specialists to fix some of the damage to the upholstered furniture. I shook my head, glad that none of the damage I'd suffered was beyond a few missing or broken pieces of dinnerware and my dignity.

THIRTEEN

"SO, YOU LOVE THE MOKA COFFEE."

I kept dicing the celery in front of me and glanced at Roy. "I know you're a coffee noob, but yes, it is undoubtedly the best coffee-brewing method on the planet, and I would appreciate it if you would recognize its glory."

Roy chuckled and rounded the corner of the island. "So why did you want me to learn how to use the moka pot?"

"I told you, we might have guests who want better coffee."

"Yeah, so it has nothing to do with Seb absolutely loving this style of coffee, right?"

I feigned innocence. "I have no idea what you're talking about."

"I think you know my roommate better than you

let on. But he's pretty tight-lipped about it too, so one has to assume it's juicy. You should have seen his face light up when he saw the moka."

He tilted his head, but I kept my eyes on my knife.

"Well, for the record," he said, "I like you both. And you meet my approval."

That made me grin at my knife, and Roy walked away, chuckling. "Someday . . ." he declared.

We continued to work, putting breakfast dishes away, when the door upstairs slammed open and loud voices echoed down the hall. Will and Xavier, another deckhand, turned the corner into the galley and whooped.

Roy slowed and looked at them. "What's up?"

Xavier, who was normally a pretty quiet and reserved Frenchman, beamed. "We got our tip in, and it's a fucking big one!"

We looked at each other and a grin slid over Roy's face.

Will bumped his hip to Roy's. "Check your email."

We both dried our hands and pulled out our phones. Sure enough, I had gotten an email from Dom and a transfer notification. The amount made my eyes bug out.

"Every awful, terrible thing I said about those people was totally worth it." Roy marveled.

I snorted.

"It's horrible that they can just pay their way back into our good graces," Xavier said. "But honestly, I don't care. I don't care one tiny bit, and neither does my bank account."

"We"—Will paused and slapped his hands on the counter—"are going to celebrate. Dom's already approved a crew night out. Like, really fucking out. It's Friday night, we're flush, young, and gorgeous. We need a fucking party."

"Way to make me feel old," I teased.

"Shut it, Marce. You're one of us. Even our ancient captain is a silver fox." He whispered behind his hand. "Don't tell him I said that."

"Where are we going?" Roy asked.

"Drinks and nosh on the Riva," said Xavier. "Then picking up the water taxi to Bačvice for a beach club. No dress code, 'cause we're all bums out of uniform. But it's a dance club with cheap shots."

"Who's staying behind?" I asked. Xavier was the newest on the exterior team, so it was likely he'd be staying behind.

Xavier shook his head. "Dom volunteered, as did Clarissa."

Clarissa had a boyfriend working on another

yacht, and Dom was probably going to call his kids, so neither was a surprise.

"Be ready at eight." Both men danced their way out of the galley. Roy and I grinned at each other and got back to our work. Xavier hadn't mentioned Seb staying behind, and now that we'd circled back to a friendship, maybe it would be nice to spend some time with him, and the rest of the crew, off the clock and out of uniform.

"HEY."

I glanced over my shoulder where Cat stood at the entrance to the galley.

"You just about done here?" she asked me.

"Yes, what's going on?"

"The girls have taken over the master cabin to get ready for tonight." She shrugged. "It's a little girly, but we've opened a couple bottles of wine and put some music on. Come join us."

Flattered, I grinned. "Sounds fun."

"Roy, you want to join us?"

"Thanks, but I'd rather not be the token gay." He wrinkled his nose and stuck his tongue out at Cat. "Besides, Seb and I get ready together. And I'm going to rub it in your face: I only need half an hour, tops, so have fun in hair and makeup!"

Cat stuck out her tongue at Roy. "We'll see you soon, Marcella." She disappeared out of the room.

"Go ahead. I can finish up the last bit," Roy said, taking the dish towel I was using to dry cookware.

"You sure?"

He rolled his eyes. "I did just say that it takes me a half hour to get ready. Not that you need a lot more time," he quickly clarified. "But you should go have fun."

"Thanks." I dried my hands off on my apron. "See you on deck!"

I gathered a few things from my room and carried them into the master cabin. The female half of the crew was spread out, girls standing at the mirrors in the his-and-hers heads, putting on makeup. Bottles of wine—I counted four empty ones already—littered the desk, which had been turned into a makeshift bar. And clothes were draped over the backs of chairs and along the bed.

"Yay, Marcella's here!" Harper squealed.

I laughed, surprised by her excitement. "Uh, thanks?" I opened a wardrobe and tucked my three dress options on the rod next to fluffy bathrobes.

"She's happy because we get to pepper you, the newbie, with questions now," Cat explained. She held up two bottles. "Red or white?"

"Red please. Questions?"

"Yes." Harper took a swig of wine. "Like, marry, boff, kill."

"Marry, boff, kill?" I repeated. I took a seat on one of the beanbags that had been pulled into the room next to Cat's chair.

"Yep, who of the crew, present company excluded, would you marry, boff, or kill? If you have to choose one."

"I'll go first, take the pressure off Marcella." Bok wrinkled her nose in thought. "Marry: Dom. Boff: Xavier. And kill . . ." She tapped her chin and named the second steward. "Paul. Because then one of us would get a promotion, probably."

"Oh, it's on, girl." Caroline, another stew, made a finger gun and aimed at Bok. "I'd fight you for it."

"So bloodthirsty." Bok giggled. "You next."

Seb's name was mentioned a lot in the marry or boff, and I fidgeted anytime someone brought him up, nervous that someone would betray their real feelings for him or cause drama. But mostly the marry and boff was ignored; instead everyone cackled over the kill and its ridiculous reasons.

"Toby, because once he told me he preferred Miller Lite beer."

"Gio. I am so goddamn tired of all the football talk."

"Will, who can honestly not fold a napkin for the life of him. Seriously, don't ever let him fold napkins for the guests."

"What about you, Marcella?" Cat turned the attention of the room to me, and it seemed to get a little quieter.

"Ah well, I guess Roy and I get along pretty well."

Harper bit her lip. "Um, but, he's gay."

Cat snorted and rolled her eyes. "Yes, that's what is keeping us from marrying these guys."

"Maybe I want to change my answer," Bok announced. "Dom is a great father, but Roy's fun. I think that's a good idea, Marce. Who would you boff?"

I hedged for a moment, trying to land on a safe answer. "Probably Dom?"

Cat held my gaze while she sipped her wine. "He's kind of a safe choice, isn't he? More mature, probably better than most of the younger guys."

My knowledge of Seb's skills flashed into my memory, and I looked away. "Kill . . . oh, Mrs. Granger!"

Harper shot wine out her nose and the whole room erupted.

"Oh, I change my answer!" Caroline called.

Bok grinned. "You're cleaning the carpet tomorrow!"

"Have a tissue," said Edie as she passed one to Harper.

Bok's shoulders shook silently and Cat looked at me thoughtfully. "Not Seb?" she asked quietly.

The laughter died from my lips. "Why?" The noise and merriment around the room covered our conversation, but I glanced around anyway to make sure no one was paying attention.

She shrugged. "He's always around and it seems to annoy you. I would think he would be on your list somewhere."

I tried to brush it off, the heat creeping up my cheeks. "Nah, he's all right."

Cat laughed. "Okay, he's definitely on your list somewhere," she said with a sly grin.

I focused on my wine. He was on my list somewhere. . . . I just couldn't decide where.

FOURTEEN

AT EIGHT O'CLOCK WE GATHERED ON THE AFT DECK OF *Themis*. The sun was somewhere behind Marjan Hill, but the sky still had a rosy glow.

Despite the no-dress-code policy, we were all wearing our best clothes: collared shirts, short dresses, strappy sandals. When I climbed out of the stairwell, several of the crew wolf-whistled.

I was wearing a floral flowing dress that Cat had helped me pick out. My shoulders were bare, my long hair down in loose waves, and I'd put on light makeup. Getting ready in the master cabin had been fun, taking advantage of the huge mirrors and vanities and sharing compliments and beauty products. My own had been thinned out when I moved aboard *Eik*—sharing a small cabin between two women left little room for nonessentials.

My eyes immediately found Seb. He was dressed casually preppy, with boat shoes and a teal polo shirt. His hair, usually tousled and loose, was slicked back with a wave and a side part.

His gaze slid over me appreciatively, a soft smile on his lips before he turned away, making my stomach flutter. The way we looked at each other felt different suddenly. Off the clock, we were no longer at odds.

Mingling at the stern, crew members leaned against the railing or stood in clusters, sipping drinks and laughing. Dom came down the port-side stairs and called out when he saw us. "Look at my stunning crew!"

There was a chorus of callouts. "Dom, come out with us!" and "It won't be a party without you."

He made his way through the group, complimenting everyone and giving hugs and cheek kisses. When he got to me, we hugged. "You did great this week. Welcome to the crew—you passed your initiation." He winked.

Pride swelled in my chest. It might not have been the big hurdle of Natasha and Justin, but it was a relief to have the charter guests gone and a job well done. "Thanks, Dom."

"Okay, guys. Have fun, but not too much fun. Be safe, and take care of each other."

There was a chorus of "yes, Dad," and we filed down the gangway to the wharf. It buzzed with activity, people out strolling in the last of the day's light, kids running around and couples holding hands.

The Riva was a fifteen-minute walk from *Themis* and while our group moved, we spread out slightly, some of us meandering while others walked with an energetic spring to their step.

Seb fell in beside me, matching my stride. He leaned in a little close and my heart rate picked up. "You never struck me as the partying type."

"I enjoy a good beach party. Especially after the week we've had."

"Did you party much on the sailboat?"

I laughed. "No, definitely not. With sailors it tends to be early drinks and early bedtimes. Plus, toward the end, we were in really remote islands. It was hard to find a restaurant, never mind a club. What about you?"

He shrugged, his hands in his pockets as we strolled at the back of the group. "Occasional crew nights like this. But usually, the club scene just feels foreign and weird to me here. As the token American, I feel uncool."

"Uncool? What makes you uncool?"

"Europeans have a different way of dressing,

especially for nights out. And I guess, growing up in Miami, most of the Europeans I encountered were wealthy. I didn't see them out at clubs. The clubs I went to were more for the Latinx crowd."

"Well . . ." I glanced at Seb, noticing the way the polo hugged his chest and showed off his arms. "You certainly look great tonight."

He laughed. "Roy dressed me. A perk of having a gay roommate." He pinched the front of his shirt and pulled it away slightly. "This is his shirt, and it's a little smaller than what I'd wear."

"It's a good color on you."

Grinning, Seb took a sweeping look up and down my body. "You look like a model in that dress." His eyes lingered on my bare shoulders and he bit his lip. When our eyes met, his were warm and appreciative.

"Thank you." I looked down, blushing, as we walked along the Riva. I was very aware that all those memories I had of Seb, which I could call up whenever I wanted to remember what his body looked like. He had his own memories from that night. Was he remembering the way I looked underneath him?

"Marce! Seb!" voices called out behind us. We spun around to find the group had stopped at one of the cafés on the sidewalk; we hadn't noticed and had walked right past.

Seb jumped into action, helping pull over another table and more chairs. Our group of seventeen squeezed into three tables and overflowed into the corner.

"Marce." Seb pulled out a chair for me, and when I sat, he took the seat next to me. With all of us crowding in, our knees brushed. This close to Seb I could smell him, feel the hairs on his knee touching mine.

He pulled me like a magnet. I knew better, but I wanted so badly to crawl into his lap, muss up his hair with my fingers, and wrap myself around him.

To distract myself, I admired the city. The Riva at night was spectacular. The palm trees were lit up from below, the buildings' facades glowed, and each restaurant had a white awning over the outdoor seating. Across the harbor we could see *Themis* lit up in the night, miniature echoes all around her in the marina, and behind us the Venetian Tower stood out starkly against the darkening sky.

We ordered drinks and regaled one another with stories of our worst charter guests. Though few stories topped the last week, some were hilarious or downright painful. Then we shared our best stories: celebrities and the little perks we'd gotten.

"I can't say who, because I signed an NDA, but I worked on a charter for a very famous football player once. He and his very beautiful model wife swam naked off the boat." Cat sighed in memory.

"Once a retired model gave me her handbag that I complimented as a tip." Harper smiled smugly. "I still have it back on *Themis*."

Will burped behind his hand. "I once got tipped a thousand-euro bottle of wine."

"Did you drink it?" Seb asked.

"Hell no. I sold it and bought a case of my favorite thirty-euro bottle of wine and sent the rest back home."

The crew laughed, and I sipped my simple gin and tonic, garnished with juniper berries and lemon, the refreshing drink going down far too easily. While we'd drunk some on *Eik,* it had never been a party; I was going to have to pace myself.

I glanced at Seb out of the corner of my eye, and caught him looking at me. A memory flooded in of us sitting at a different bar, halfway around the world, talking over shots.

"You were always teasing me, and I thought it was payback for that first day."

Seb turned in his seat and rested his arm on the back of my stool. His eyes melted into a look of mirth. "Oh, flaquita. *I was flirting with you."*

Heat crept up my cheeks. "No, you weren't."

"Yes, I was. You're beautiful, and you were always blushing around me."

"Well, I've seen you naked. It's kind of hard not to think about."

Seb smiled wide. "Oh, you think about me naked? Every time you're blushing?"

"Ah, zitto!*" I pushed him away, hiding my face in my hand.*

Seb caught my hand and pulled me closer to him. His other arm slipped around my back, his finger lightly grazing the sensitive skin of my side, exposed by my tank top.

Our eyes met, and my laughter died. Seb's eyes were lidded, his nose carefully grazing my cheek. "I like you thinking about me naked."

We had hustled back to *Odyssey* and made coffee, Seb sobering me up before bringing me to bed, his kisses tasting of dark roast and sugar.

I put the glass down, swallowing, and felt heat that was more than the Mediterranean air.

Edie, sitting on my left, interrupted my thoughts by changing the topic to the regatta next month. "So, who's placing bets on Alex for the win?"

Roy stood up a round of drinks later. "I think"—he leaned over the table, his gaze glancing around and making eye contact with everyone—"we need shots."

"Shots, shots, shots!" Harper chanted.

Seb and I exchanged an amused look. The chant took over, and Roy and Will went to the bar to buy a round.

"I feel confident enough in Will that he'll come back with something at least halfway decent." Seb leaned in. "No buttery nipples or blow jobs."

I chuckled. "I will be curious to see what they come back with. Roy loves a craft cocktail; I just can't picture him doing shots."

"To be fair, I have a hard time thinking of you doing shots, and I've actually seen you do them."

Seb's eyes held mine and a blush crawled up my cheeks. We did shots together that night—commiserating over our jobs, such a contrast to this night.

"I seem to remember waking up not nearly as hungover as I'd expected the next morning."

"Well, we may have done a few shots." Seb sipped his beer. "But I prefer my partners to be as sober as possible."

"That's right. I made us coffee."

His eyes flicked down to my mouth. "It was only the second-best thing I ate that night."

My heart beat harder, and as if he could tell, Seb dipped his eyes down lower, tracing the line of my bare shoulders and the swell of my breasts right above my dress. He shifted in his chair and a quiet growl came from his throat.

Roy and Will returned with two trays of shots. They were passed around until we all had one. Roy cleared his throat and held up his shot. "We just learned a valuable life lesson at the bar. One should always know the local language for a toast." He hiccupped. "And some very generous gentlemen may have bought us some shots at the bar and given us some practice at toasting in Croatian. So . . ." He leaned forward and concentrated. *"Jevell . . . Je veil . . ."*

Xavier laughed. "What, are you trying to speak French?"

"Casse-toi," Roy retorted gracefully, sticking two fingers in Xavier's face.

"Živjeli!" Will cut in.

We clinked glasses and tried our own hand at toasting in Croatian before tossing the shots back. "Whoa." Seb grimaced, placing his shot glass upside down on the table. "Remind me not to drink with Croatians too often. What the hell was that?"

"Raahh . . . rakiha . . . rakija! Something like that." Roy fluttered his hand.

"Fruit brandy," Will told us, leaning over. "It's . . . pungent. And I think we are all learning that Roy cannot handle his booze. You're cut off, buddy."

Dramatically tilting his head back, Roy whined. "I can't say no when cute lads offer to buy me drinks."

Will patted him on the back. "A couple more shots and you won't make it to the club."

"A couple more shots and your roommate will be helping you puke in the head later tonight," Seb muttered under his breath.

"Fair point, mate." Roy waggled a finger at Seb and looked at him through narrowed, though slightly unfocused, eyes. "Don't go getting pissed and being irresponsible."

"I would never." Seb grinned.

Roy turned his attention away, and I leaned in toward Seb. "Has he actually gotten pissed and thrown up?"

"Nah," Seb said. "He's too good of a kid for that, really."

"A kid? He's older than you."

"Well, maybe I'm a kid too, then."

Under the table, I crossed my legs, letting my foot hook under Seb's calf. "I hope not."

Seb gave me a hungry look and, with a deep inhale, slid his hand under the table and squeezed my knee.

Anticipation curled in my stomach.

WE'D SOBERED ROY AND A FEW OF THE OTHERS UP WITH food and water before picking up the water taxi at the wharf at the Riva. Our group wedged into the small boat, and I sat delicately on the corner of a seat. The speedboat shot off into the darkness, and Seb's arm wrapped around me, bracing me and preventing me from falling off the edge of the seat as the boat rocked in the bay. His fingers pressed into my stomach, tracing small little circles through the fabric.

Bačvice was a small, shallow beach a few bays over from Split's main harbor. Our little taxi made the turn into the bay and we could see the party going in the corner, lights strobing and the thump of the bass carrying over the water.

We disembarked and followed one another through the front door. It was loud and packed, people wall to wall, and Toby, walking in front of me, quickly disappeared. Just when I thought I'd lost our whole group, I felt a tug on my arm from behind. I looked back to see Seb and he pulled me in close. His mouth to my ear, he said, "Want to dance?"

I gazed into the next room, where a DJ stand was

set up and bodies writhed. I looked back at Seb and he took my hand and pulled me with him.

The Europop music faded as Seb pressed me into his body. It had been years since I'd been to a dance club, and I didn't do shots often, and I definitely knew it was a bad idea to let Seb look at me that way. But the club was crowded, our friends lost in the scene, and so we danced.

There was no pretense. We were in each other's space right away, one of my arms wrapped under Seb's, my palm spread on his back, the other hand at the back of his neck, mussing up his hair. Seb guided my body, a hand on my hip, fingers gripping and kneading while we moved to the beat. My stomach fluttered, my eyelids dipped, and I focused all my attention on Seb.

Before long we were sweaty and rumpled. My forehead was pressed to his neck, and all I could see was the glimmer of the dance lights reflecting off the sheen of sweat on Seb's throat. I wanted to lick it.

My body was loose and pliant, Seb easily moving us with the beat. One of his legs had migrated between mine, his thigh pressing into my center. The friction was building tension already, and I ached.

I could feel the tension building in Seb, too. His hands roamed, fingers dragging up and down my thigh, big hands spreading over my ass, a thumb stroking the side of my breast just under my arm.

And a glorious weight rested against my hip.

I closed my eyes and called up my memories: Seb raising my leg up onto his shoulder, the way he had stared down at us as he thrusted inside me, the curve and roiling of his muscles. I could feel those same muscles under my hand right now, and I just had to touch his bare skin.

The moment I slipped under the hem and onto the bare skin of his stomach, Seb pulled back. Bereft, I opened my eyes and locked them onto Seb's.

"Let's go home."

I nodded.

Seb grabbed my hand, tugging me off the dance floor. When I realized we weren't headed for the door, I pulled back on Seb's arm. "Where are we going?"

"We need to tell the crew we're leaving."

My face fell and I pulled my hand out of Seb's. "I don't think that's a good idea."

Seb studied me and then nodded. "Let's at least go check in. We'll make up an excuse. Come on." He pushed me ahead of him in the crowd but didn't pick up my hand again.

We wound our way through the people, occasionally spotting one of our crew members here or there, dancing with each other or with a stranger. The bulk of the group we found out on the patio. The night air was refreshing on my skin, and a breeze helped lift some of the sweat-dampened wisps off my face.

Cheers went up. "Marcella! Seb!"

"You disappeared!" Harper shouted.

"Dancing," I called back. I caught a flash of movement out of the corner of my eye and turned to the shadows of the patio. Roy was pushed up against the wall, a tall, muscular guy doing the aggressive pressing, their mouths fused.

I eyed the situation warily. "Is he sober enough for that?"

Will tossed a glance to the couple, brow furrowed. "Yes, he hasn't had a drink since we got here."

Twisting my lips, I debated.

"Don't worry, Marce. I'll make sure he's okay."

Picking his glass up, Will gave me a little smile before taking a sip. His eyes returned to Roy.

"I'm going to head back to *Themis,*" Seb announced, plucking up his shirt and fanning himself. "Anyone else want to go grab the water taxi with me?"

"Yeah, I'm off." Xavier downed the last of his drink.

"Me too," said Edie.

I chewed my lip nervously. No one was going to

suspect anything, right? I looked around and no one seemed to be assuming anything about Edie and Xavier.

"Marce?" Seb called.

I swung my gaze back to Seb. "Yeah, me too."

A flash of relief crossed his face and I ducked down to hide my smile.

"Yeah, all right, let's go, then." Seb waved us out, retreating under a chorus of goodbyes.

FIFTEEN

BACK ON *THEMIS*, THE LIGHTS WERE DIMMED, AND WE moved about the deck quietly. I stepped toward the aft stairwell. "Good night, everyone."

"We're right behind you," Xavier said.

"Oh well, I'm going to my cabin."

"Yeah." He shrugged. "I'll cut through the guest cabins instead of through the front staircase." He gave me a perplexed look. "Is that okay?"

"Yeah, of course." My eyes flicked to Seb's and he covered his mouth with his hand. Was he laughing at me?

I took the stairs, feeling the weight of everyone behind me. At the turn, I called out again. "Good night."

The door closed behind me and I waited. Where was Seb? Would he go to his room, wait an appropriate amount of time, and then come to my room? Or should I go to him? Roy was still out. Would Roy come home tonight and notice Seb's empty bed? Or would he be out all night with his hookup?

My room was too small for pacing. I sat on my bed, tapping my thighs and fidgeting. Belatedly, I realized I should probably brush my teeth, wash my face, and clean myself up a little bit.

The toothbrush handle was sticking out of my foamy mouth when my door opened. Turning around, I saw Seb click the lock in place before scanning the room for me. His hair was damp and tousled, water droplets dotting the shoulders of his shirt. Seb's eyes landed on my bewildered face and he coughed.

"Uh, whoops. I didn't brush my teeth."

I shrugged and continued to brush mine. In the mirror, I watched Seb come up to the doorway to the head. He stretched his arms out above him, placing his hands on the top of the doorframe.

"Honestly, I'm a little disappointed to not come in and find you stepping out of the shower naked."

I squinted at him and he chuckled. His arms dropped and he stepped forward, coming up behind me.

"This little freckle right here." He touched a lone spot on my shoulder, one that was normally covered by my sleeves. "This little freckle has been torturing me all night."

He pressed his lips to the spot, letting his tongue dart out and taste my skin. I broke away from him, bending over to spit into the sink, and he laughed. But then he dropped his hands to my hips, and while I was bent over, trailed the back of his hand over my butt.

The hem of my dress tickled my legs as he played with it. I cupped my hand, rinsing my mouth as fast as I could. Just as I put the toothbrush back in its holder, Seb flipped the skirt of my dress up and pulled my hips back toward him. My hands went out, bracing myself on the counter.

Now that I had my voice back, I choked out, "I can't believe you're trying to seduce me in my head."

He ignored me, grabbing two handfuls of ass cheek and giving them a good squeeze before letting them go. I arched my back for him and he groaned softly. Then he planted his palms on my ass and wiggled them around a little bit.

"Did you just jiggle my ass?" I asked, incredulous.

"Your ass is fantastic," Seb said, keeping his eyes on my butt.

"I'll take that as a yes."

In the mirror I watched his face. He stared in the

kind of way teenaged boys stare in wonder at their first nudie magazine. I opened my mouth to tease him, but instead I gasped when he slipped a finger under my thong and across my slick skin.

"Oh Jesus." Seb removed his finger and I whimpered. He tugged me upright and spun me around, pinning me against the sink. Seb's fingers threaded through my hair and his lips crashed down, swallowing my surprise.

Seb kissed me like it was for survival. I fought him back, pressing myself against him and straining to get closer. Weeks—no, months—of remembering the way his body felt had brought me to the edge and I teetered, trying desperately to find what I was looking for.

Seb eased our kisses to gentle flutterings and walked backward, leading me into the cabin. In a swift move, he had my dress up and over my head and his mouth latched onto my nipple. Looking down, I ran my fingers through his hair, soft and drying. It was long enough that I could fist it, if I wanted to.

My gaze shifted to his eyelashes, closed in reverence while he kissed and sucked. The scruff of his beard rubbed against the underside of my breast. It would be red and irritated in the morning but so worth it.

I tried to hike a leg up onto Seb's waist, but he pulled back and stripped his shirt off. He undid the buttons of his shorts and kicked those off too, before reaching down and pulling me up to wrap my legs around him.

Our lips met again and Seb put a knee on my bed, guiding us onto the mattress. He laid me down, fitting his body over mine, and slowed our kisses.

With only the soft fabric of our underwear between us, we ground into each other. His fingers traced over me, running up my sides, down my arms, lacing our fingers together.

He pulled back for a breath, giving me slow little kisses. "God, I could kiss you forever."

"Please don't."

His chuckle vibrated from his chest to mine, and he bent down again.

Seb was in charge. Our kisses rose and fell, set by his pace. We tested each other out, nibbling, licking, sucking, remembering the ways we liked it. He groaned when I nipped at his lip, and I gasped when he shifted his weight, his erection pressing into just the right spot. He repeated the motion, rolling his hips over and over again.

I broke away from his mouth and buried my face in his shoulder. The tension was building and my legs were tightly wrapped around his, keeping him right where I needed him.

His breath ghosted along my neck, warm and quick. His hips snapped and he pressed forward harder once.

Suddenly his weight over me was gone.

"What . . . Seb?"

Picking up his shorts, he rummaged through the pockets until he pulled out a foil wrapper. He tossed it onto the bed and then climbed back onto his knees between my legs. "How would you like to come?"

"What?" I propped myself up on my elbows, my knees closing together slightly.

"Nope." Seb put his hands on my thighs and forced my legs open wide. "How do you like to come? My hands, my mouth, my cock? What do you want, Marce?"

My eyes rolled back. "Cock, definitely cock."

"Attagirl."

Seb grabbed the side of my thong, tugging it out from under me and hoisting my legs up to get it off. He rolled to the side and quickly stripped his boxers off before putting the condom on.

He climbed back into position, pinning my thighs with his hands. His cock rubbed up against me, slick and hard but not quite at the right angle. Reaching down, he adjusted and eased himself in.

My head fell back onto the pillow with the slow stretch of my body around him. Seb muttered, *"Dios mío,"* before thrusting in fully.

"Fuck, Marce, that is so hot." His eyes were wide and wild, his body straining.

One elbow came down beside my head, and Seb threaded his fingers through my hair, propping my head up for a kiss. He pressed our foreheads together, staring at me while he flexed and pumped.

"Like this?" he whispered. I nodded and he grinned at me. "Lost your words, Marce?"

I nodded again and he laughed before kissing me. When he broke away, his eyes dipped down to watch us again. I looked down too, over the planes of Seb's chest and abs. Tilting my hips, I rested the back of my thighs on his, giving us an even better view.

Seb's pace picked up, his words frantic little whispers.

"Tan bueno . . . Estás preciosa. . . ."

I closed my eyes, my stomach tensing up as he hit just the right spots. Seb trembled with effort. "Marcella, please."

A couple more strokes and I was over the edge, clenching around him. Seb's fist closed around my hair, tugging almost to the point of pain, and the combination of everything brought tears to my eyes.

He was mumbling words I didn't understand, trying to ride it out, tight and tense.

My breath caught in a shaky, nearly violent inhale, and then everything relaxed. Seb grunted and resumed his strokes, chasing his own orgasm down. His mouth came over mine in deep, wet kisses until he tensed, legs scrambling on the bed and cock pulsing. He gaped, gasping and holding eye contact until he quivered, relaxing back into the cradle of my legs.

We both caught our breath, breathing hard, our hearts racing against each other. A tear fell out of the corner of my eye, and Seb's face dropped.

"Marce, oh shit, did I hurt you?"

He immediately tried to untangle his hands from my hair.

"Seb, stop, it's okay. It wasn't that, I promise."

He relaxed, but still carefully pulled his hands out of my hair.

"Are you okay?"

I nodded.

"Ha. Words please, Marce. You scared me there."

I swallowed as Seb traced a finger over my collarbone. "Yes, I'm okay. Way better than okay."

He grinned at me and rolled us gently to the side. Reaching down, he pulled out, making sure the condom came out too. He stood up and walked into my head, closing the door. The cool air washed over my skin, giving me goose bumps. My heart was still racing, breaths still ragged; did he have to get up so soon?

The water ran in the head, the toilet flushed, and Seb reappeared. Resting his elbows on the bed, he leaned over and gave me a soft kiss, my misgivings falling away.

"Can I stay?"

SIXTEEN

Roy and I spent our entire last day in Split provisioning. While I knew there would be plenty of supplies in Corfu, Split was a bigger city, and it was better to grab as much as we could here before leaving. Roy and I made careful notes, going through our list and writing down things we were having trouble finding.

It was good to have the distraction, something else to think about other than Seb. He had climbed back into bed with me the night before and cradled me to sleep. That morning, he had woken me gently, caressing and kissing until he slipped inside from behind, a slow and warm session before I'd even opened my eyes.

The memories kept popping into my thoughts, no matter how busy I was. But they didn't linger long.

Between food deliveries, we also made two days' worth of crew meals. One set we divided up into portions and put into the fridge. The next morning, we would leave early for Corfu, spending all day out at sea. We'd arrive into Corfu at night. Weather conditions were not ideal, and seeing as it was only one day at sea, Roy and I pretty much had the day off, and staff were left to reheat their own meals.

Roy scrubbed dishes as we ran through my menus for the Boyds' visit. Since he had been with the boat when Natasha and Justin had bought it, he'd assisted the previous head chef during several of their visits.

"What about the crew tomorrow? Who gets seasick, what comfort foods should we put together?"

"Will's actually the worst, so we probably won't see him much of the day. He stays in his cabin, even though I tell him he would feel better up top. Everyone else does pretty well. Clarissa eats like a horse, so she'll want stuff to nibble on throughout the day. Dom likes crisps at night. Umm . . ."

"How about ginger snaps or something like that?" I asked.

"They'd get eaten, I'm sure."

"What do you like to do at sea?"

"Usually just read in my bunk. Seb will be in and

out all day, so it's all very interrupted. Although . . ." Roy put a clean dish down and leaned toward me. "Seb didn't come home last night. Which is odd, because as drunk as I was, I was pretty sure he came back before I did."

I didn't say anything, but my lips twitched trying to hold back a smile and a flush crept up my cheeks. Dang it, Seb was right. There was no sneaking around without Roy knowing.

"Oh. My. God." He put both of his fists to his mouth. "I knew it. He is *so* into you." He slapped a palm over his mouth. "Oops, shit, I didn't say that."

Now I had a full smile on and couldn't help myself. "Well, I'm pretty into him too."

"I won't say anything, I swear. I actually can keep a pretty good secret."

I gave him a skeptical look.

"My family didn't know I was gay until I was eighteen. That was pretty impressive, honestly."

I laughed. "Okay, I'll give you that one."

"Did you hook up on your last boat too? Seb would never tell me."

Seb was a better secret-keeper than I was. A nervous flutter went through my belly. Maybe Seb knew better than to tell Roy. They were best friends—how had he not told him? "Well, then I'm not going to tell you either."

Roy pouted but picked the dishes back up again. "Fine. My point is, the next time Seb doesn't sleep in his own bed, I'll back you both up."

I squeezed his forearm. "Thanks, Roy."

I WAS UP BEFORE THE SUN, INTENDING TO HELP ROY with a fresh breakfast for the crew, but he shooed me out of the galley.

"Go watch them leave the dock and get the sails up," he suggested. "It's pretty cool."

While we had briefly sailed with the charter guests on board, I hadn't had time to enjoy the view. I climbed to the main deck and took a seat on one of the aft couches, where I could see the entire boat. The deck team was running around, prepping lines and putting gear away. I felt the ship rumble to life underneath me, the engine starting up. I hadn't put my earpiece in, but I got to listen to most of the conversation anyway while the crew discussed getting off the dock.

Marina staff on the wharf helped us untie our lines and then threw them back to our crew. Slowly, the stern of *Themis* pulled away from the wall. Early-morning passersby stopped to watch as Dom smoothly maneuvered her away from the dock.

With *Themis*'s bow pointed out to sea, the crew filtered away until there was just Edie and Toby on deck. Together, we watched as the sails unfurled as if by magic. Everything was electronic—so different from what I'd seen on *Eik*. The masts pivoted as we passed the entrance to the bay, and *Themis* picked up speed. Within a few minutes, we had our engines off and were coasting along.

Conditions weren't incredibly calm, but *Themis* was so big, it was nothing like what I'd expected. I stood up and wandered along the deck, casting my eyes up to the sails often. The square sails, if you could ignore the carbon fiber around them, made it look like we were on a historical ship from the 1800s, a weird way to feel on this modern, tech-savvy superyacht.

Standing at the side rail, I looked over and watched the water rush past.

"It's pretty cool, right?" Seb sidled up to the rail and joined me.

I tore my eyes from the sea and nodded at him. "It's a bit different from what I was expecting, I guess."

"Nothing like *Eik*?"

"No, totally different," I said. "She moves a lot differently in the water."

"My first sail on *Themis* was my first sail ever."

I turned to face Seb. "Really?"

"Yeah. It's kind of this beautiful, peaceful thing. I didn't think I would like it, but I do."

"Is that why you want to do that sailing coaching?"

"Yeah. I'm really racking up my sea time for my licensing, but I like the idea of diversifying a little bit. I'll never be a professional skipper or tactician, but perhaps I can get my sailing endorsement and more job opportunities."

"What's a tactician?"

"It's the person who plans out the strategy, plots the course. The Boyds fly a professional tactician in for when *Themis* races."

We stared down at the waves for a few minutes.

"I've got some time off before my next shift. You?"

The wind whipped hair into my eyes, and I pulled back and smoothed my hair down. "I'm pretty free today."

We eyed each other.

Seb cocked his head. "I can be down at your room in ten minutes?"

I glanced up and down the deck. No one was out here to see us. Seb glanced around too, and when he found no prying eyes, he slipped a hand around my hip and squeezed. I glanced up at the bridge deck, but we were on the aft side; Dom and whoever else was up there would likely be facing forward. "I have two hours off. Let me come to your room." The rasp in his voice made me shiver.

"Okay," I said, taking a deep breath. "See you in ten."

"I SPENT SOME TIME . . ." SEB PANTED. "AFTER YOU left . . . trying to convince myself that we weren't as good as I remembered."

He had just pulled out of me, and my heart was still racing, my sweat cooling my skin. I swallowed and let the words hang for a few moments and then gasped out, "Yeah?"

Seb's head wobbled against the bed. "It's just as good as I remembered. Between us."

He rolled to sitting and paused at the edge of the bed, his shoulders rising and falling. Adjusting to the slightly tilted floor as *Themis* sailed along on a lean, Seb made his way into my head and closed the door. A few minutes later he came back out and I bounced on the mattress as he collapsed facedown next to me again, blocking my escape from the bed.

With his face scrunched up into the pillow, I barely caught his grunt.

"That was pretty vigorous," I said.

A finger poked me, the accompanying voice muffled. "Go clean up so we can nap."

I rolled over onto Seb, my front to his back, his ass fitting neatly into the curve of my pelvis. He flexed his butt cheeks, and I giggled.

When I came back, Seb was looking slightly more rejuvenated. He opened an arm up and I climbed over him to nestle against his side, my cheek pressed against his chest.

"So we're doing this?"

My heartbeat picked up again, nerves making my stomach flop.

"Doing what?"

Seb shifted under me. "I guess . . . this isn't a one-night stand? Well, a two-night stand, if we count Antigua?"

"No, it's not."

I tilted my face up to look at Seb, and we both waited.

Finally I broke and propped my head up on my arm so we could talk. "I shouldn't, because it's unprofessional and so risky, but I like being in bed with you."

He gave me a soft smile. "I like it too."

"But let's keep it between us, yes?"

Seb ran a hand over the scruff on his face, his eyes

searching the ceiling of my cabin. "Yeah," he finally said. "I think that would be best. Except Roy will probably figure it out."

"Maybe."

Seb looked at me skeptically.

"I'm more worried about Dom," I said. "He sleeps in the next room over. Thank goodness there's a hallway between our cabins, and he spends so much time up at the helm anyway."

Seb shrugged. "If he catches me in the hallway, I'll just say I was headed to check the gear in the utility room. I don't know how I'll explain to Roy when I'm gone every night, though."

My eyebrows rose. "Every night? That's ambitious."

"At least it's pretty safe when we are at sea. Roy might not be paying close attention to my schedule, since I've got night watches and Dom's almost always at the helm. Sometimes he even sleeps up there while someone else is on watch." Seb grinned mischievously. "I might have to gag you when we're in port, though."

I smacked his chest. "I'm not that loud."

"Not yet." Seb laughed.

"Cocky."

"Mm-hmm. So this is temporary?"

I thought for a moment. "We're seeing this

through. Obviously there's tension here"—Seb wiggled his eyebrows at me, and I grinned—"and we need to get it out of our system."

Seb nodded, looking thoughtful. "Your contract only goes to the end of the season, right?"

"Yeah. Yours?"

"Yup."

"Are you going to stay if they'll have you?" I asked.

He took a deep breath. "I'm hoping a promotion will come up. But I might have to look elsewhere."

"Ah," I said. It was a harsh reminder of another reason why we couldn't be in a real relationship: within a few months, we might be watching each other sail away again.

SEVENTEEN

It was nearing dusk, and we would be in Corfu when I woke up, so I took one last chance in daylight to wander the boat. I had camped out in my room all day, naked, alternating between napping and Seb's visits. He had snuck in a few times, first for a quickie, but then using his hands and his mouth to make me pliant and satiated before he slipped out the door for his shift. Then he'd returned with hot food, woken me up to eat, and repeated the whole thing all over.

When I finally did get up, I roamed the bottom deck of *Themis,* checking in with the crew who was awake, and then went into the galley. It was fairly clean, a few stray dishes here and there. Opening the fridge, I found about half the meals gone, so the staff had been well-fed.

Climbing up the stairs, I emerged onto the main

deck. The sky had grayed with low clouds, and the wind had picked up a bit more. Our sails were still flying, and *Themis* clipped along at a good pace, occasionally taking a wave over the bow. It was past sunset, and on a clear day we would have all been out on deck enjoying the start of the night.

The deck was bare, and I cut across and pulled the doors open to slip inside. On the couch in the lounge, a handful of the crew was watching a movie.

"Hey, Marcella, howzit going?" Roy called out.

"Good. How are things up here?"

"Easy, easy."

"Is everyone feeling okay?"

"As far as I know. I checked on Will a few minutes ago and he's a bit green but he's held it down all day, so that's good."

"Who's on watch right now?"

"Dom's up at the helm."

"All right, I might go up and check on him."

"Oh yeah. If you haven't been up there while we're underway, you should see it."

I left them to their movie and climbed up the atrium stairs to the bridge deck. The wide windows provided a 180-degree view of the clouds and grayness surrounding us. Dom sat in a black leather chair in front of the instruments, doing something on his phone.

"Evening, Dom."

Dom looked over his shoulder. "Hey, Marcella. How's your day been? Haven't seen you much."

"I kept to my room, mostly." I stood in front of the electronics and took it all in. "Wow, this is an intense amount of information here."

Dom stood up, tucking his phone into his pocket. "Want the grand tour?"

"Sure."

Dom walked me through most of the panels. Some things I recognized from previous boats; others were foreign to me. On *Odyssey,* I rarely ever ventured onto the bridge deck. But the helm of *Eik* had often been the center of activity. I had held my own watches while everyone else slept, learned how to use the gear on board, even helped out when there was trouble.

One item I recognized was the chartplotter. While it wasn't the same one *Eik* had, it was similar and I could navigate around it well enough. I pointed to the screen, glancing up just before touching it. "May I?"

"Sure." Dom gestured for me to go ahead.

I touched the screen and zoomed out, trying to get a sense of where we were. We were entering a narrow strip, land on either side, and I looked up and out the window. Shouldn't we be seeing the coast?

Dom followed my gaze. "The clouds have our visibility blocked. But mainland Greece is somewhere out there."

I zoomed out further, and saw that to our starboard side should be the heel of Italy. I wavered my finger over the screen before resetting the view.

We moved on and Dom showed me the controls for the sails and for the masts. I didn't understand much of the terminology. *Eik* had had just two sails most of the time, a mainsail and a genoa. Neither looked anything like *Themis*'s sails.

"Have I lost you?" Dom asked.

Pressing my hands to the counter, I blew out a breath. "Yes. Wow, this is such a complicated boat."

"She really is." We wandered back to Dom's original chair and he hauled himself up before gesturing to the chair next to him.

"How are you finding things here so far?"

The chair had foot- and armrests, so I adjusted myself to sit comfortably and then folded my hands in my lap. "Things are pretty good, despite the terrible charter. I like your crew."

Dom's chest puffed out with pride. "Glad to hear it. I think they've all done pretty well. Roy working out okay?"

I nodded. "He's very competent and easygoing."

"Good. It's always felt to me like the head chef

and crew chef have to work more closely than anyone else on the team."

I let my eyes wander out over the ocean. "I agree. But I also think we're used to much higher-pressure jobs. No offense intended, but this is a cakewalk compared to the normal restaurant."

Dom's phone buzzed and he pulled it out to check.

"Do you need me to go?"

He waved a hand at me. "No, it's just my daughter texting."

"How old is she?"

"Twelve and starting to think about boys, unfortunately. Her mum is being pretty lenient and . . ." He sighed. "It's hard to be okay with these kinds of things going on when I'm not there."

"Are you the kind of dad who would threaten boyfriends?" I grinned.

"Absolutely. Those boys wouldn't know what hit them." He laughed, but it quickly faded to a sigh. "I hate that I'm not around much."

"What happened, if you don't mind me asking?"

"Ah well," he started, "we met on the job, of course. Where else are you going to meet someone in this field? It was fine for a while. Most yachtie couples are dramatic as, but Diane and I did pretty good. We got married, and I was optimistic that we'd just keep on like we were. But I was a young, dumb kid. Diane wanted family and so we moved back to her home in England and I tried to work in one of the ports, but it just lacked something."

"I know exactly how that feels. It's like working in a restaurant. There's something missing because you never leave, never see anything."

Dom blanched. "It was really too late for me to be a port captain, so my pay was shit compared to what I get here. And now I've got child support and what-not." He shook his head. "There's no winning, really."

"Sorry to hear about your troubles."

"Ah, it's okay. I got to fly them down here once already, and Nat and Justin let me keep the girls here with me on the boat. Actually, this was just before you got here. They slept in your cabin while it was empty."

"Aw, cute little sleepover." I gestured to his phone. "Do you have photos?"

Dom gleefully pulled up pictures of his daughters, Ashley and Maura, and we flipped through them for a while, Dom telling me funny stories about the girls.

"What about you?" He leaned back and tucked his phone away. "You're single. I'm assuming I would have heard otherwise."

"Yes." I bit my lip. Technically not a lie.

"The dating pool around the yachties is just a minefield, isn't it? These young kids aren't so level-headed, and it's the worst when it goes south, having to lose two crew members at once. They make me feel old."

"I just try to avoid the drama."

"What about those guys on the sailboat?"

I startled. "In the Pacific?"

"Yeah."

"God, why does everyone think I was with one of them? Definitely not."

He shrugged. "You have to really like people to be stuck on a small boat like that. It's one of the things I've always been asked about: How do you stand being cooped up in here?" Dom spread his arms out. "Like this is tough, nineteen crew on a huge yacht. I can't imagine five crew on a fifty-five-footer."

"Well, nothing ever happened. Not with me, anyway, but yeah, two of the other crew members."

"Was it bad?"

"It was just okay. Part of the reason I left. But I heard it got worse after I was gone. To your point, she was younger and didn't take it very well."

"There's always one in the couple who can't handle it." He shook his head. "I know you're more experienced than most of these crews, so you know better. They're all young and think with their dicks—excuse my language. I can't believe how many times I've had to mediate between a couple because they're fighting or teaming up on others. Honestly, aside from being away from my kids, it's the worst part of the job."

My stomach was a lead weight inside me, full of guilt. Why did I think Seb and I were special, that we'd come out the other side of this with our jobs still intact? It had already backfired on me once. Maybe I was setting myself up to learn the same lesson the hard way.

EIGHTEEN

THEMIS HAD TOO DEEP OF A DRAFT TO FIT INTO THE marina at Gouvia, the main one on Corfu, so we anchored outside in the bay. It wasn't an easy stop for the crew—being at anchor and so far from the main town would make things harder—but fortunately the weather forecast looked good for the next week, a few days prepping for us and then through the Boyds' visit. It could have been worse: taking the dinghy back and forth to shore with provisions or laundry was exponentially harder in the rain. Instead we looked forward to a few calm, sunny days at anchor.

When we connected to Wi-Fi in Corfu, Seb had an email waiting for him from the regatta. His application to the sailing coaching program had been denied.

"I just . . ." he started, running his hands through his hair and tugging. "I've been doing this job for a few years now, and I'm still a deckhand. I need something to give me an edge for a promotion."

"You're great at your job," I told him. "And at least you are getting sea time in now, right?"

"Yeah, my sea time is good. I almost have enough to qualify for my captain's license. But that's just a piece of paper." He shook his head. "I need someone to take a chance on me." He closed his eyes. "My contract is up at the end of this season, and so is Derick's. He's a great bosun, and I like working for him, but, man . . ." Seb clenched his fists. "I want his job."

I swallowed thickly. "What will you do if he renews?"

Seb turned his head to look at me. We watched each other, a few heavy moments hanging over us. Seb broke first, turning away.

"I don't know, Marce. I just don't know."

My stomach plummeted, and I chided myself. Our jobs were temporary. Our relationship was temporary. My whole life was temporary. I shouldn't forget that.

Dom picked Justin and Natasha up from the airport the afternoon of their arrival. I had a simple Italian dish to prepare for the evening, a tuna puttanesca made with locally caught fish. Will was pairing it with a light Zinfandel and Roy had baked a boule to serve alongside.

When Justin and Natasha were comfortable on deck with pre-dinner cocktails, Dom called me up. I climbed the stairs, nervously smoothing down my chef's jacket, with Roy right behind me.

I caught sight of Natasha first. She was petite and of Asian heritage, with long jet-black hair pulled up tight in a ponytail. Just like I remembered, she was lithe and immaculately dressed. She stood at the rail of *Themis,* looking out toward the sunset, a martini in her hand.

She turned and spotted me approaching. "Marcella." Her smile was warm and welcoming, and she had a soft British accent.

We shook hands. "Pleasure to see you again, Mrs. Boyd."

"It's lovely to see you too. We are most excited to be here on this culinary weekend."

Roy peeked around behind me and greeted Natasha with a warm hug and air kisses.

Justin joined us, touching Natasha's elbow as he came up behind her. He towered above her, his hair fiery red and a mischievous grin on his lips. He greeted me with air kisses. Most of my communication had been with Justin, so I was immediately more comfortable with him. Roy hugged him too, relaxed and casual with the couple.

"How are you finding things on *Themis* so far?" Justin asked me.

"Excellent. I knew coming in that Dom would be a joy to work for, and I'm glad to say I've been right."

"And how has our Roy been treating you?" Justin slapped him on the back.

"He's proven to be a great crew chef so far."

"Excellent. We're looking forward to this weekend. Nat's been extremely busy at work, and I'm just happy to be out of the house a bit more."

I had researched the couple prior to committing to the job, and knew that Justin had been a stay-at-home dad, and continued not to work even after their children had grown. Thus, he took care of more of the personal matters for the couple.

Justin winced. "I heard about the messy business with the charter."

Roy didn't sugarcoat it. "It was rough, but we pulled it off."

"Well, here's to Natasha and I being less of a wreck." He sipped his drink, amber liquid in a tumbler.

"We're happy to have you," I said. "Do you have any questions about the menu for tonight?"

I recited the menu and the Boyds assured me it sounded good, and Roy and I departed back to the galley. We were still a few hours from dinner service, so we worked together to accomplish the prep work and clean as we went.

The call for dinner came around eight thirty, later than I was expecting. I plated up the dishes and sent them upstairs with Bok and Caroline. I followed fifteen minutes later to stand by for feedback.

Dom sat at the table, dining with Justin and Natasha. When I crested the stairs, the discussion centered around the next day's plans.

". . . walking through the Old Town and Esplanade before it gets too warm."

"Mr. Boyd, Mrs. Boyd, how is dinner this evening?"

Natasha looked down at her plate and my heart skipped a beat. "Marcella, of course I was excited to have you cook a traditional Italian meal, but perhaps a puttanesca was a poor start. I find the sauce too salty for my taste, and it could be smoother. Unless I'm mistaken, the pasta is from a box?"

I took a big breath, eyes wide. "Yes, ma'am."

"I understand that we're going more casual in concepts than we might be for a special event or a charter guest, but I still expect the dishes to be sublime. A simple sauce base is not going to cut it. Please, brighter flavors"—she gestured with her fork—"and really, let's push the limits here."

I forced myself to exude confidence. This job was ideal, I was an excellent chef, it was just a minor setback and teething pains. "I completely understand. Would you prefer something else?"

"No, we will continue with this. It's good, Marcella." She cupped my elbow. "It's just not as good as it could be."

I turned to Justin, who swallowed his bite and looked up at me. "I'd like a word with Will, too. I like the reds a bit bolder than this one. The bread is excellent, as expected."

As eager as I was to please the Boyds, and as much as their criticism stung, I dipped my chin. "Roy made the bread, sir."

Justin grinned. "Please pass along my compliments."

Taking the stairs down, I wondered how I could turn this around. It was only the first night, and the Boyds' disappointment sat like an anchor in my belly as I appeared to have fallen short.

NINETEEN

Before retiring, I dug deep and pushed away my guilt at the subpar performance and set to redeem myself. I rewrote the entire menu for the next day. No, not rewrote, replanned. We were still going to serve the same dishes—a warm pasta with confit and vegetables, but I would make it more distinguished, better. While I sat in the crew lounge, reworking the menu, Seb passed through.

He did a double take when he saw me. "Marce, what are you doing up? The Boyds are in bed already."

I didn't look up. "Dinner was nearly a failure. I need to rewrite some plans before bed."

Seb took a thorough look around and, seeing no one except Roy at the sink, slid into the booth next to me, pressing his side against mine.

I compared my inventory notes. Did I have enough parsley to tweak the tartare recipe?

Seb's arm came up around my back and kneaded my far shoulder while I flipped through my paperwork. Three bunches in the walk-in and I needed enough for the lamb.

After a few moments Seb's fingers pressed in deeper and hit a knot above my shoulder blade. I lost focus on my paperwork and leaned my head to the side for a just a moment. . . .

Reflexively, I twisted my shoulder out of Seb's reach and squirmed. "Seb! I have to get this done. Go away."

He laughed in disbelief. "I know. I'm just trying to help you relax."

"I don't need to relax. I need to get this menu finished!" My frustration leaked out with my words, and even though I knew Seb was trying to be supportive, the clock ticking away was stressing me out.

"Hey." The admonishment from the doorway was Roy. His eyes bounced between Seb and me, and the tension in the room deflated.

"This is my job, Seb," I said softly, looking up at him. "It's high stress sometimes."

Roy shuffled away, and Seb ran a hand through his hair, eyes downcast.

"I know. And I'm a distraction, right?" The corners of his mouth quirked, and he glanced up.

"Usually you're the best kind of distraction."

That got me a smile.

"Look," he said, leaning back against the seat. "You are really good at your job. Tomorrow's going to go a lot better than tonight. I know it. Just don't stay up so late that you can't function well tomorrow." Seb wrapped a hand around my head and pressed his lips to my forehead.

"Okay, old man."

The wisps of hair escaping from my bun tickled as he huffed a laugh. "Back to work with you. Night, flaquita."

I worked for a while longer, the sounds of Roy cleaning keeping me company. When he finished, he sat beside me, and I showed him my revisions.

"Anything I should change?" I asked him.

He pursed his lips, flipping pages. "Nah."

My head fell back. "Thank God. Let's call it a night."

I trudged through the empty guest quarters. When Natasha and Justin stayed, they preferred to sleep upstairs in the bridge deck cabin instead of down below. It was nice to be able to take a shortcut when the Boyds were here, although I knew that the next visit would also bring Alex with them and I'd be back to climbing the stairs, walking across the deck, and then back down the stairs by my cabin.

After a quick shower, I stumbled into my bed. My mind kept spinning, my body exhausted but unable to sleep. I rolled from side to side, visions of fresh pasta and basic sauces troubling me.

In the morning I woke up bleary-eyed and groggy, but I quickly got to work. The Boyds were very traditional with their breakfast, and early risers. Roy wasn't up yet, so I had the quiet kitchen to myself, folding doughs and dicing fruit. I was no pastry chef, but I knew my fresh baked goods were delicious and worth the effort now.

Catarina passed through after a half hour. "Natasha and Justin are up doing yoga on the bridge deck. Can we have breakfast in thirty?"

"Absolutely."

Thirty minutes later I was trooping up the stairs with Percy and Bok behind me. We had beans, sausages, eggs—fried for Justin, poached for Natasha—croissants, toast, spreads, and whipped butter. Will had already been through for freshly squeezed juice and I could find no fault in my meal preparation.

The day was crisp and muted, the sea state calm. Somewhere out to the east lay mainland Greece, but for now it was awash in the glimmer of sunrise.

The bridge deck cabin was a smaller cabin with

big sliding glass doors looking aft, and huge windows giving them the best view. The doors were thrown open, lounge furniture pushed back to make room for yoga, and the dining table was seated with service for two. Catarina had set the table with elegant flowers and clamshell folded napkins.

A small bar cart was set up to the side with juices, coffees, and teas, and Will attended the Boyds. I paused to the side, waiting for Natasha to finish her chat with Justin and acknowledge me. She caught sight of me over Justin's shoulder and smiled.

"Good morning," I greeted Justin and Natasha. "Your breakfast."

I laid the dishes in front of them. Natasha's eyebrow rose, taking in the presentation I had made. The bread, freshly made this morning, was thinly sliced and branded with *Themis*'s scales of judgment. The slices were pinwheeled out, the eggs nested in the center on a bed of beans, with wilted tomatoes and herbs fringing the toast.

"Marcella, this looks fabulous."

I suppressed a smile and bowed my head. "Thank you." I stepped back, feeling a hundred times lighter, energy flowing through my body, and left Justin and Natasha to their meal.

When I returned downstairs, Roy was in full swing prepping the crew meal, and we worked together, cleaning and prepping, until Catarina and Bok returned with the empty plates. Completely cleared-off plates. I smiled in satisfaction.

"Well," Catarina remarked upon dropping the dishes off, "I'd say you did very well for the full breakfast. It is Justin's favorite meal of the day, so A-plus marks, Marcella."

My shoulders relaxed, my breath escaping from me in a relieved rush. It was good to hear that Cat, who knew the Boyds much better than I, thought I'd hit the mark. It made the late night last night worth it.

The crew was filtering in, picking up something to eat as they woke up or passed through. Seb entered the crew lounge and poked around for breakfast.

"How was this morning, Marce?" he asked.

I grinned, much more relieved. "They loved it."

"Hey!" Seb jerked forward for a moment as if he'd hug or kiss me, but with Cat still standing nearby, he quickly corrected and offered me a high five. "I knew you could do it. You're gonna kick some ass this weekend."

"Thanks, I hope so. You want some coffee?"

Seb eyed me. "Yeah, I do, but you've been up for a few hours already, and don't you have a few hours off? I think I'm driving Natasha and Justin to shore at ten. Roy can make me coffee. You can go take a nap."

"Umm . . ."

Roy came up from behind me. "Nah, we've got this for now. You definitely deserve a nap. I'll make Seb coffee, and when you come up, I'll have a nice one made for you, too."

"Don't you dare. I'll make my own coffee, thank you very much."

"Hey, I need the practice or how am I ever going to get better with that confounding pot?" Roy chuckled.

Seb put a hand on my back, guiding me out of the galley and into the hall. "Go nap," he commanded. A flutter of excitement went through me. I liked the tone of his voice, the command that was bossy but caring.

I sighed on my way to my cabin.

Distractions.

TWENTY

I DID NAP, SETTING AN ALARM FOR FIFTY MINUTES TO just get in a power nap. When I arrived back in the kitchen, Roy had done a massive amount of prep work for me, and I found much of my mise en place completed.

Hours passed while I created plate after plate of hors d'oeuvres, some needing to chill or marinate for a few hours. I became entranced by my work, a one-woman show crafting, tasting, perfecting.

Roy bounced around me, barely on my radar as he made the crew meals. He had an hour off in the afternoon, and combined with the rest of the staff doing a comprehensive cleaning while Justin and Natasha were ashore, I had a blissful calm in the galley, and even when the Boyds returned, they only took a minor tea service from the staff that the stews could handle.

Seb entered while the lounge was empty, and walked purposefully through the galley, turning his head to make sure we were alone.

"How's it going up there?" I asked.

He shrugged. "As usual, Natasha's in the office on a conference call she couldn't get out of and Justin's out reading. We're gearing the water toys up for a swim when she's off the call."

I nodded and held up a spoon. "Try this."

Seb eyed the green sauce on the spoon, but leaned forward and closed his mouth around it. He winced and swallowed. "Ugh, Marce, mint?"

"You don't like mint?"

"I hate mint," he said.

"But you're always so minty fresh. Who doesn't like mint? It's not like I fed you cilantro."

He grunted and rubbed his belly. "I love cilantro."

"You are weird."

"Mint things are always green desserts, and, like, leave the healthy green crap out of my dessert, okay?"

"Right, never mind the sugar and heavy creams." I winked at him.

"Speaking of sugar." He tugged at my elbow. "Two minutes," he said.

"Wait, wait, wait." I finished the last row on the tray and set the piping bag aside, before letting Seb pull me away from the counter and wrap his arms around me.

I straightened my back and tried to stretch, stiff from bending over the trays and piping out choux pastry puffs and macarons. Seb's strong hands reached around behind me and kneaded my muscles. I fell limp against him.

"Now, I'm not trying to get in your pants," Seb teased.

I ducked my face into his neck. "I know. I shouldn't have—"

"It's all right. I know you are under a lot of pressure. But it smells amazing in here, and the dishes are looking beautiful. I know you have a long night ahead of you, but you'll be great."

We stood like that for as long as we could, until the door upstairs opened and sunlight and voices echoed down the stairwell. Seb pulled away, giving my shoulder one last squeeze. I sighed and bent over again, picking the piping bag back up.

Time flowed around me, and sometime later the call on the radio came in that Justin and Natasha were ready and we were upping anchor bound for Petriti. The scenery outside my window changed, but I barely noticed.

The anchor dropped, the stews came in and bustled around, setting up the table for dinner service, and I fielded questions over silverware and place settings. Justin and Natasha had sundown cocktails on the bow, and I checked the table on the main deck.

Catarina had perfectly complemented the meal with modern votives and local fresh flowers. Will was mixing craft cocktails, also tasters for the regatta event.

I sidled up to Catarina. “Any last-minute advice?”

She shook her head. “I’ve been keeping an eye on you all day. Natasha will love the croquembouche, and the menu is diverse. I think . . . I think they will like it.”

With my nervous energy and barely contained excitement, I wanted to hover, just to be *sure* the spark was there when Justin and Natasha saw the setup. But Cat had shown her confidence in me, and I wanted to support her, too. I forced myself to leave.

Back downstairs I discovered a new quote on the whiteboard.

“Hard work should be rewarded with good food.” —Ken Follett

"NATASHA MAY BE THE MOST INFURIATING PERSON I'VE ever worked for."

It was two a.m. and my declaration was met with looks of sympathy from Cat and Roy.

"She's—" Roy began.

I rounded on him. "She's what? Particular? Frustrating? So goddamn picky?"

The dishes were nearly done, and I had a list of notes for almost every single dish I'd served tonight. My menu had been good—really good—but Natasha was pickier than any chef I'd ever worked for. And some of the notes were asking for a trial-and-error approach. *Would this be better with au jus instead of bone broth? More subtle flavor on the lavender.* And *Let's rework all of this for tomorrow.*

Instead of a meal out, as originally planned, I had to repeat the whole thing all over again. Perhaps not the whole thing—some of the dishes Natasha had found satisfactory enough not to remark on. The only compliment I received was on the langoustine with caramelized endive and kumquat-sake gelée, about which Natasha remarked, "Heavenly."

Okay, at least I had one real winner of a dish.

"Natasha is incredibly particular in all aspects of her life. She's been wildly successful in doing so, and she can afford to demand the absolute best," Cat said soothingly.

Justin, at least, had been more enthusiastic, finishing off each of his plates.

The menu sat in front of me on the counter, and I braced my hands on either side and reread my notes. A lot of these things, I had to admit, were Natasha's personal preferences, and she had every right to have her own opinions. I struggled heavily with valuing my performance tonight. I had plenty of experiences in restaurants, cooking for a wide variety of people. Many times, I had worked under a head chef, but it had been a few years since I'd answered to no one but myself—and guests. But guests were less fickle as a collective, and Natasha was used to personal chefs and cuisine that, I begrudgingly admitted, was perhaps beyond anything I'd experienced.

In other words, Natasha might be an Everest of a client.

Cat hugged my shoulders, gave me words of encouragement, and retreated for the night. I was in a bind. I needed to come up with another tasting menu, tweaking most of the dishes while still working within the confines of what I had on board.

I inventoried and then bent over my notes, continuing to plan until daylight broke and Roy shoved me out and to bed.

THE SECOND NIGHT OF TASTINGS DID GO BETTER. Natasha's notes were slowly tipping more toward the positive and less toward corrections. I made detailed sheets of notes, and by the end of the evening—midnight again—Natasha pushed back from the table.

"This is enough, I believe. Marcella, do you understand the direction to move from here?"

"Yes, ma'am. Our notes will suffice and I think the menu is looking pretty firm now."

"Good. Justin and I are going to retire for the evening. We'll see you in the morning for our post-yoga breakfast."

"I'm looking forward to the beans and toast again." Justin smiled at me.

I nodded. "Thank you. Have a wonderful evening."

I gathered the plates and descended the stairs, where I found Roy and Seb in the galley. Seb stood by the coffee machine, chatting while Roy washed the dishes that had piled up in the sink. When Seb turned and saw me, a grin tugged on his lips.

"Ah, Marce, you look like shit."

"Hey," I protested weakly.

Throwing the last of his coffee back, Seb handed the mug off to Roy. "Come on, it's bedtime. Roy's going to clean up."

"You don't have to do that. I can clean my own —" My argument was voided with a giant yawn.

Seb plucked the chef's cap off my head and gently spun me around to untie the knots of my apron. He rotated me again and worked on the buttons down the front of my jacket. Instead of watching his fingers nimbly work their way down my chest, I watched his eyes.

The jacket and apron were tossed into the laundry under the counter with the dirty towels and Seb pointed me toward the door. "Come on, Marce."

We walked aft through the guest cabins and back to my room. "I don't need an escort," I grumbled.

Seb laughed behind me. "I've still got some time before my night watch starts, so I'm going to make sure you fall asleep instead of lying awake."

"How are you going to do that? Mind control?"

My body was tugged backward, Seb pressing my back up against his front. "A hot shower, a little massage, and I think you'll be out like a light," he whispered into my ear.

In my cabin he roughly stripped me down and pushed me into the shower. The heat started to ease the ache in my back and hands from the cramped work I'd been doing all day, but I couldn't be bothered to move and scrub myself.

A few minutes later—maybe? Had I fallen asleep

standing up?—Seb turned the water off. "Good enough," he murmured, and pulled me out, wrapping me in a towel and scrubbing my skin dry.

He guided me to bed and down onto my stomach. I breathed deeply and closed my eyes. Having someone to care for me, someone to look after me and make sure I didn't work myself to death . . . that was new. And I was glad it was Seb.

TWENTY-ONE

SEB WAS COOING SOFTLY IN MY EAR, AND STRONG COFFEE wafted under my nose. I groaned and cracked open my eyelids.

"Morning, sunshine. I've got a coffee for you."

The surface of the coffee was coated in the thick foam of cremina. I sat up. "Did you make this?"

Seb chuckled. "Dios mío, no. Roy made it."

I took a tentative sip and blanched. "My God. How does he make coffee so poorly?"

"He should stick to tea."

I nodded and rubbed the sleep from my eyes. "What time is it?"

"Time for breakfast service soon. Roy's making the bread, but I think it's best if the rest was up to you."

"Okay. I'll be up soon. Hey, what happened to my massage last night?"

Seb laughed. "I started your massage and you snored!"

I rolled my eyes. "I think that means you owe me one," I teased.

Seb kissed my forehead and whispered, "Rain check, then," before disappearing, leaving me to choke down the coffee and get dressed on my own.

Roy had put most of the ingredients I needed out on the counter and had been prepping while the bread baked. "Thanks for the help, last night and this morning."

He shrugged, and I noticed the circles under his eyes too.

"God, what is it like when they stay for a week? Is it always this crazy?"

Roy shook his head. "Not usually. They have high standards most of the time, but also know when to tone it down. And they do like to eat out a lot."

I hummed and got to work. Roy pulled bread out of the oven while I diced fruit and prepared the beans, saving the eggs for last.

When we got the call, Roy fried, I poached, and we had their breakfast up the stairs minutes later.

"Good morning," Natasha called when we reached the top of the stairs.

"Morning." Justin tipped his mug at us.

"Your breakfast." I slid Natasha's plate in front of her and then walked around to present from the correct side for Justin. Roy set the accompaniments on the table. "Would you like anything else?"

"No, thank you. But we're leaving shortly after breakfast and won't bother you downstairs, so these are for you both." Justin gave us each an envelope. "Thank you very much for the service this weekend. We look forward to seeing you both in a few weeks' time."

"Thank you, sir." I shook their hands and Roy and I retreated downstairs. Back in the galley, I pulled the envelope out of my pocket. "What's this?"

"Tips," Roy explained. "The Boyds work with Dom and like to hand out the tips in cash, personally. Thankfully, for us, they're pretty generous."

"Nice." I pocketed the envelope again, looking forward to seeing how much my stress over the weekend had been worth.

I opened the envelope later in my room. A lot. My stress had been worth a lot. The tip was generous, and when it was added to my tip from the charter and my substantial salary, all my hard work was worth it. Especially when we got to celebrate.

WE HAD A FEW DAYS BACK AT THE ANCHORAGE OUTSIDE of Gouvia for cleaning and recovering. But Wednesday had been marked on the calendar for a week: *fun day at anchor*. It was Dom's treat to us for a job well done while Natasha and Justin were here, and though I wasn't particularly keen to slack off, Seb convinced me to take the day off too. And truthfully, it would be an easy week—we were staying on Corfu and waiting for the delivery of a few parts and toys for the boat. Roy and I still had to feed the crew, but we'd have time for fun, too.

Seb was sitting on my bed that morning, naked and sleepy. "Please come out and play with us."

"Seb, I've got a lot to do before the regatta."

"But . . . bikini. Wet slippery body." He pulled me between his legs. "Sunbathing."

"Are you just in your own little world? This is not the 'Swimsuit Issue.'"

He pouted. "Just a little bit of fun, Marce. You deserve it; you worked so hard this past week."

"I did work hard." Seb pulled my head down for a kiss.

"You worked hard and I deserve a treat. . . . I mean, you deserve a treat." He grinned wickedly.

I slouched against him. He was hard to say no to. "Fine, I'll come have fun. So mean."

He laughed and then spun me and gave me a gentle push. "Bikini, now. Sneak preview."

Bending at the waist, I pulled open a drawer and plucked out a matching bikini set. "This?" I held the two pieces up against my naked body.

Seb nodded, eyes wide and eager.

Gripping them by the strings, I tossed them over my shoulder and sauntered into the head, closing the door.

"Hey!" Seb protested from the other side. "I wanted a show."

"Go get dressed in your own room," I called back.

"Tease," came his muttering through the door, and I laughed. I caught a glimpse of myself in the mirror—I looked happy and carefree. This Marcella, out of her uniform and with a hot lover in her bed—she looked good.

A HANDFUL OF THE CREW WAS OUT ON THE MAIN DECK and dressed for the water. A nice benefit of not fitting in the marina was that we were anchored outside the bay in the clear blue waters where we could swim and play. I carried a platter of fruit up with me, which I put on the outdoor dining table.

The yachties had pulled together loungers and

beanbags from all over the boat—everyone picked their favorites—and the hodgepodge was gathered just under the aft mast.

"Oh, fruit! Thanks, Marcella." Harper plucked a pineapple slice and bit into it.

I eyed the empty drink glasses scattered around, and noticed Bok's flushed face and Derick lying limp in one of the loungers. "I have to make sure no one's drinking too much on an empty stomach. Does anyone want a smoothie?"

"Roy already offered, but thanks," Bok said. "We want you to have fun with us!"

"Thanks." I stripped off my cover-up and sat down on the beanbag next to Harper's chair. "Where is everyone?"

Just then Seb padded around from the gangway, dripping wet. His board shorts stuck to his skin, and his face lit up when he saw me. His grin turned sultry as his eyes dipped down over my body.

Harper and Bok looked at each other and giggled.

"Hey." I gave Seb a little wave.

"Hey, Marce. You gonna come swimming with us?"

"I will in a little bit."

He nodded. "Harper, do you mind?"

She stood up from her chair. "Go for it."

I watched curiously as Seb grabbed a line that I

hadn't noticed before. It was looped around the rail and led up to the very bottom corner of the lowest "yard"—nautical speak for the horizontal parts of the mast, according to Toby. I stood up to take a better look.

Stepping up onto a footrest pushed against the side, Seb carefully climbed over the rail and found his balance. He gripped the knotted line and counted to three before jumping off the rail and swinging out over the water.

He let go and flailed with a Tarzan-like shout before flopping into the water. When he surfaced, I heard Roy's voice shout, "Dude, four points for the landing, but I'll give you an additional two for the gay scream."

I peered down the side of *Themis* and found Roy and several other crew members floating just off the gangway.

"That was not gay. Your floaty is gay."

"My floaty *is* gay," Roy retorted. "Literally, Seb, gay. It's a fucking rainbow unicorn."

"I like your unicorn," I called down.

"Thanks, Marcella, but I don't share Rodrigo."

I mock-pouted at him.

Seb stage-whispered, "Dude, let your boss ride the unicorn."

Harper had used a boat hook to retrieve the line. "You gonna take a turn, Marcella?"

"Do it!" Seb called.

"Marcella! Marcella! Marcella!" Roy started the chant, and soon everyone down below was in on it.

"Yes, yes, fine." I grabbed the line from Harper and everyone cheered. The encouragement over something as simple as a little rope swing—something that didn't really matter in life—it felt more powerful than the support for my food. *Take this rope swing—you're one of us.*

"Just don't lose your bikini top," Bok advised. "You'll never hear the end of it."

"Boo," Seb called.

I rolled my eyes at him and he stuck out his tongue.

"Okay." I climbed up like I'd seen Seb do and looked down at the water. It wasn't very far down, not like some jumps I'd made off other boats. *"Uno, due, tre!"*

I swung off the rail and out over the water. When I hit the peak, I let go and crossed my arms over my chest, weightless and free for a moment before plunging into the sea. Straight-legged, I shot down, and then hung suspended for a moment, noises muffled and distant. The water sent chills over my body and pushed me back toward the sun.

When I broke the surface, the group cheered.

"Seven points, Marcella," Roy quipped.

"Minus two for not losing your top," Seb chimed in.

I splashed him. "Perv."

Seb blew a kiss at me. "Come on, there's a two-person floaty lounger. Let's grab it."

We climbed aboard the tethered inflatable and drifted along. I shifted my head to look at Seb, and eyed the drops of water on his golden skin. His chest rose and fell with every breath, and the water droplets wiggled and sparkled in the sun.

His elbow nudged me. "Stop staring. You're going to make me hard, flaquita."

I grinned and closed my eyes, relaxing back on the headrest. The crew continued to laugh and chat around us, punctuated by the occasional splash of the rope swing. Seb and I kept our distance, but I felt every inch of the space between us.

And then I felt more than just air. One of Seb's fingers had wandered closer and was lightly tracing the edge of my bikini bottoms.

"What are you doing?" I whispered out of the corner of my mouth.

"No one can see me." His finger slipped under the seam.

I glanced up at the deck, and yeah, maybe no one was paying attention.

"Besides, your staring was more obvious than this."

"My staring?" I said, mock-insulted.

"Yeah, you were practically drooling, too."

"I was not."

"I had to wipe drool off my shoulder."

"Liar!" I shoved Seb, and his weight shifted, unbalancing our whole lounge float. Seb gripped the edge for a comically long moment before splashing into the water. He disappeared completely, and I leaned over the edge of the floaty, looking for him.

The far edge rocketed up, tipping me over into the water face-first.

We played like that for a while, knocking each other off, rating everyone's rope swings, and Roy wandered over in Rodrigo and knocked against us for a while, chatting.

The sounds of an outboard engine crept closer, and when Seb shifted, I looked up too. Toby drove the dinghy, motoring up to the gangway with two other passengers.

"Where's he been?" I wondered.

"He told me he was going hiking."

Toby navigated around our float lines and pulled the tender alongside the gangway. A man hopped out and tied off and then helped a woman step out of the dinghy.

"Everyone, this is Nan and Bryce. Since none of you lot were willing to go hiking with me this morning, I had to make some new friends. Come on, I promised them lunch, and you should hear their story."

Seb and I glanced at each other. He shrugged, and leaned over to tug the line and pull us in.

TWENTY-TWO

Despite having a day off, we all needed to eat. Roy and I pulled out platters of meats and cheeses and laid them on the outdoor dining table.

Nan and Bryce, still wet from the rope swing, joined us for lunch. The two Americans were a bit younger than I was, and very polite, thanking us for the food and gushing over what fun they were having. They both looked around at *Themis* wide-eyed, and Toby promised them a tour once we'd all dried off.

"What do you both do in Corfu?" Seb asked.

"We work on a sailing yacht," Nan said, "but a much smaller one."

"Oh, like one of the charter boats?" Bok asked.

Nan took a bite of her sandwich and Bryce chimed in. "No, it's privately owned. We don't do any charters, but we're a full live-aboard crew. The owners fly in for a few weeks at a time, then we sail the boat somewhere ourselves, and they fly back in again."

"So it's just the two of you?" Seb's eyebrow ticked up. "Is that hard?"

"Not really." Bryce slung an arm around the back of Nan's chair. "We're used to it by now. It's been, what?" He looked at Nan. "Three years now?"

"How often does your owner fly in?" I asked.

"Maybe about half the time. He gives us a pretty free rein to get the boat where he wants it, so we usually have a week or two to make the sail, depending. They just flew out four days ago, and the weather looks pretty good to leave Monday for our next stop, which is Sicily, and then the owner flies in to meet us in one week."

"That's pretty good. I'm assuming you do all the maintenance and stuff yourselves. It's like you are cruising but with fancier guests regularly."

"Yeah, it kind of is." Bryce laughed.

"And you guys"—Seb pointed back and forth between them—"are a couple?"

"Yeah. Boats this size typically look for a couple to run it. A captain and a chef."

My eyes met Seb's across the table. He leaned forward, his interest sparked.

"I think it's the opposite in our industry," I said hastily. "Having couples leads to unnecessary drama. You know, breakups and picking sides. That kind of thing."

Or worse. Sailing was an isolating experience, and that could be exploited. Mia, a sailor I'd met in French Polynesia, had made a few comments that led us—the crew of *Eik*—to believe her ex-husband had been abusive.

Bryce nodded, thinking. "For us, it's better because we are a team. If couples have longevity and if we're proven to work together, then it's a pretty good gig. We originally met while working for a charter company. We did work as a couple on crewed charters for a while, but since I've got a background in racing, we got a job offer from a former charter guest who went on to buy his own boat, and the rest is history."

I wondered if they had made sacrifices. Nan wasn't a trained chef like me, but had she given up something to follow Bryce? Had he?

Working as a captain on a private boat was Seb's dream job, but did he have other requirements? A certain size boat, or a destination?

"Tell us about your boat," Seb said, snapping me back to the conversation.

They were on a twenty-meter performance cat, a

brand I'd never heard of. Edie got Bryce onto the topic of rotating masts and the electronic controls, while Nan leaned toward me and we talked about long passages. I told her about my experiences on *Eik* and sailing through the islands.

"What do you do on *Themis*?" she asked me.

"I'm the head chef." Pride infused my voice, which made me hesitate for a moment. Had I ever been this proud of my job?

"Oh, that's great." Her eyes were wide. "How fancy does it get here?"

"Pretty fancy. But *Themis* is one of the most luxurious boats I've been on. She's one of a kind." I doubt Nan's galley had any of the luxuries mine did. In fact, I bet it was more like *Eik*'s, and I shuddered to think about giving up my space and toys.

"That's amazing. I did some basic cooking skills classes through the charter company, but our owners like more home-style meals." She waved off her skills humbly. "They love to fish, and that seems like half my job when I'm with them, taking care of the things they catch."

"That is one thing I miss about the cruising I did. We don't fish very often on *Themis*. We've got too many mouths to feed, and charter guests, at least the ones we had recently, aren't interested. But we are so fortunate to have a lot of fishermen we can buy from in every port."

"Did you work in restaurants, too? Would you go back?"

"Yes, several throughout Europe." I pursed my lips. "I haven't really thought about what I will do next. Maybe someday I'd go back, but for now, I like this lifestyle. It forces me to be more creative, more flexible. Unless you are the head chef with a nightly menu, there's not much creativity in restaurants."

"It's hard to beat the traveling," Nan said, smiling.

I looked out over the water to the boats at anchor around us and the island of Corfu rising out of the sea. My job was tough, but a good kind of challenge. And I was getting paid to tour the world now. This was exactly what I wanted; I just had to make sure I held on to it. "It sure is."

SEVERAL CREW MEMBERS WERE GOING OUT FOR THE evening, but Edie had declared it a movie night.

"We're watching *The Princess Bride* and ordering pizza. If you don't like it, you can fuck off," she had announced.

We'd all had drinks at the bar—poor Will only got

a partial night off—while Edie set up the movie. *Themis* didn't have an entertainment room like many of the other yachts I'd worked for, but Roy swore to me that the setup was even better.

I watched from below as the rig was adjusted. The mast was rotated so the yards were perpendicular to the boat. Then a single square sail rolled out, creating an enormous projector screen.

Seb and Roy returned with the pizzas just after sunset. We all trooped up to the aft lounge deck and claimed our chairs. Seb flopped onto the double-wide lounge and patted the spot next to him.

I looked around, but no one seemed to be paying any attention or cared where we sat, so I eased myself down and propped up my feet. As the day faded, boats around us lit up, masts blazing and hulls glowing in the night. Speakers were set up around the deck, so we watched Princess Buttercup escape the Sicilian in surround sound.

The next thing I knew, Seb was gently shaking me awake.

"Marce, wake up," he whispered. "The movie's almost over."

I was curled up on my side, a leg thrown over Seb's and my head on his chest. I sat up quickly, but our double lounger was a little bit farther back than everyone else's chairs, so no one seemed to have noticed. A blanket lay stretched across our laps too, covering us both from the cool Mediterranean air.

Resting back beside Seb, I settled down in my seat again. "Thanks for waking me up."

"Sure. You were about to miss the best part anyway."

We watched Princess Buttercup have a ridiculously long fall from the castle window, and then she and Westley rode off into the sunset together and shared the most romantic kiss in history.

Seb twined his fingers with mine under the blanket. I wished for the rest of the crew to disappear so I could lean over and kiss him. It was so romantic here, with a beautiful island behind us and the stars above. The only thing that would make it better would be Seb's lips on mine.

TWENTY-THREE

ANCHORING OUTSIDE A MARINA HAD ANOTHER downside besides having to dinghy back and forth to town—every night at anchor the deck team had to take shifts. Seb and I spent less time together now.

As *Themis* bobbed out in the harbor, I'd go to bed after we'd cleaned up from dinner service. Seb would take a nap in his own bed, do his watch in the middle of the night, and then sneak in to join me in my bed when he was off his shift.

But one night I thought, *Why go to bed?* Instead I worked on my provisioning list and supplies for a little while in the crew lounge until everyone had gone to sleep except Toby, who was on watch. He passed through occasionally for a midnight snack or while doing his rounds.

"Can't sleep?" he asked me once.

"Nah, not tired enough yet. Figured I'd get some work done."

"Cool." He nodded and wandered off.

Later the door swung open and instead of Toby, it was Seb. He startled when he saw me. Glancing around quickly, he checked to make sure we were alone.

"What are you doing up, flaquita?" He leaned over the table, planting a slow, long kiss on my lips.

When he pulled back, I blinked up at him, my breathing coming ragged. "I thought we'd hang out on your watch."

Seb's eyes warmed. "You didn't have to do that. You need your sleep."

"Right now I'm getting plenty. But I might curse you out when we're knee-deep in the regatta."

He grinned at me. "Acceptable. You know I do have to actually do stuff."

"Yeah, I thought maybe I could tag along?"

"You can tag along anytime you want," he purred.

"Perv." I smacked his shoulder and climbed to my feet. "What's first?"

Seb wasn't kidding. First he led me up to the helm, where he took notes on the boat's position, the wind conditions, and the radar. We pulled out a rangefinder and he showed me how to measure the distance between us and other boats. "We have to make sure no one's going to drag into us or vice versa."

"That was always a concern on *Eik*. We only did anchor watches a few times when the weather was bad, but I know Jonas was always worried."

"It has always amazed me about how many smaller boats actually do drag anchor. It's scary watching someone's boat just fly backward and you don't know if there's anyone on board or what. And then when they hit another boat . . ." Seb shuddered.

We went downstairs to the main deck and walked a loop around the entire rail. Despite us being alone, the boat was still brightly lit. I had assumed that someone would turn off the mast lights and underwater lights when we all went to bed.

"Nah, they pretty much stay on all the time," Seb said when I asked. "It makes us more visible at night. And have you ever noticed the light at the top of the mast? It's hard to see from here."

I looked up and tried to shade my eyes against the brightness of the mast lights. "No, what's up there?"

"A flashing red light. We have to have one for air traffic. We're so tall, airplanes have to watch out for us."

"What? That's crazy."

He laughed. "Yeah. Funny how on most superyachts—non-sailing ones anyway—even though they are bigger, they aren't taller. You don't have masts, so you would never think about something like that."

"What next?"

"Well, normally when we are at anchor, we've got guests on board, so I have to clean. But since we don't have guests, things are pretty tidy right now, and Toby probably got a lot of the day's dirt."

"So, what do you normally do when you've got free time at night?"

"Hang out in the pilothouse. Wanna come up with me? Or should you go to bed?"

"Nah, I'll come up."

We climbed the stairs and entered the helm again. Seb checked his watch. "I have to do another reading on the hour, and I prefer to keep the lights off so I can see better."

"Oh really? I would say it's nice and romantic, but the glow from these instruments makes us look pretty ghoulish."

Seb grinned. "Ooooohhhh! I'm a ghost. Coming to eat you." He tugged me to him, pulling our hips to touch, and his lips chased mine, bending me back for a kiss. I gripped his collar, opening up for him and sliding our tongues together. Seb groaned and pulled me harder to his body.

When we broke off, we were both breathing hard, and I nuzzled his nose until I caught sight of the captain's chair, dimly lit in the darkness. Placing a hand on Seb's chest, I pushed him back. I tilted my head. "Take a seat, Captain."

Surprise swept across his face, and then delight. "Oh yes, ma'am." He stepped up into the captain's chair and settled back. Patting his lap, he asked, "Are you going to join me?"

I stood in front of him, shook my head slowly, and dropped to my knees.

Sucking a deep breath in, Seb stared at me, wide-eyed. "Holy shit. This is the biggest fantasy I didn't know I had."

He tried to help me unzip his shorts, but I swatted him away. His dick was hardening, his chest starting to heave in anticipation. I pulled him out and enjoyed the feel of him on my palm, hard and heavy. I placed a kiss on the tip, then moved my way down his dick, gliding my lips gently along his soft skin.

Resting my head on his lap, I gripped him with my fist, sliding a thumb up and down the head as he leaked.

"Oh God, Marce," he groaned. His knees spread a little wider and he squirmed in his seat.

I kissed my way back up and licked the tip before wrapping my lips around the head. I looked up at

Seb as he threw his head back and closed his eyes. I worked his length deeper, using one hand to massage his base while the other crept up his shirt, where his muscles flexed and rolled.

"Marce, I'm coming. . . ." He grunted. I didn't pull back, but kept working him like he did for me when I was the one coming.

I waited for his breathing to calm, his heart rate to even out under my palm, before pulling back completely. When I sat back to stand up, Seb pulled me toward him and I fell against him in the chair. He plunged into a deep kiss, gently tugging my hair but forcefully slipping his tongue inside.

After a few heavy minutes, he eased back and twisted me into his side.

"That was a fucking dream come true."

I giggled as he ran a hand through his hair.

"I'm serious, Marce, a blow job in the captain's chair of a yacht—they make porn about that. But mostly, that's just what I'd love to have happen." He pressed a kiss to my lips again. "Thank you."

I leaned against him, pleased that I'd found a way, at least sexually, to show Seb how much he meant to me.

TWENTY-FOUR

"We should go into town today," Seb said while he ate breakfast leaning against the galley counter.

"Who's 'we'?" Roy asked.

Seb gestured with his spoon. "The three of us."

Roy wrinkled his nose. "What, and I'd be your third wheel? No, thank you."

To be fair to Roy, since he was the only person on the ship who knew about us, he tended to get stuck watching us act like a couple.

"I'd rather," he continued, "let you two go off by yourself. I like having the room to myself. I can get Dwayne out."

I paused my dicing to look at Roy quizzically. "Who's Dwayne?"

Seb groaned, and Roy grinned. "My battery-operated boyfriend. He's getting a lot more attention now that Seb's gone so much."

"Moving on." Seb waved away Roy's laugh. "What do you say, Marce? Lunch and some time exploring?"

"I think a few other people are going to town today."

He shrugged while putting his dishes in the sink. "It's a big enough town. I'm sure we won't run into anyone."

"Yeah?"

Seb slid behind me, pressing a kiss to the nape of my neck. "Mm-hmm." I scraped the onion I was dicing into a bowl and put my knife down, turning in Seb's hold to loop my arms around his neck.

A towel flew across the room and landed on our heads. "For God's sake," came Roy's disgruntled voice. "Get the hell out of here."

XAVIER GAVE US A LIFT TO SHORE, SEB UNDER THE GUISE of going for a walk and me to go shopping—both were true.

We waved goodbye as he puttered away from the dock, and as soon as Xavier turned, Seb threaded his fingers through mine and we exchanged a smile.

Together, we meandered through the old town, getting lost in curved streets that didn't exist on Google Maps, and Venetian buildings that, despite the variety of pastel colors, all started to look the same.

Walking past a souvenir shop, Seb jerked on my hand, pulling me into an alleyway.

"Where are we going?" I asked.

Seb pressed me against the wall and looked back toward the street. "Clarissa's in the shop across the way."

"Oh?" I followed Seb's gaze, my voice infused with worry.

But Seb had other plans. His fingers splayed against my jaw, pulling my focus back to him, and his lips brushed against mine, once, twice, and then we were indulging in long, slow kisses, my back against the stucco wall and Seb's mouth all I could think about.

A throat cleared behind him, and we broke apart, my heart racing until I realized it was a judgmental elderly man passing us.

Seb pulled away and tugged me with him.

The streets finally spit us out into the town square. Horse-drawn carriages waited next to rows of parked scooters, and the fountains were rimmed with bright pink flowers. We crossed the park and climbed the highest point of the fort, getting a view of the bay and *Themis* bobbing in the teal water.

Seb leaned against the stone rampart. "Man, if eighteen-year-old me could see me now."

I laughed, closing my eyes and tilting my face up to the sun.

"Halfway around the world," he continued. "Beautiful woman beside me. And look at my home." I opened my eyes as he gestured out at *Themis*.

"Hmm. At eighteen, I was trying to convince my mother that going to culinary school would be good for the orchard. And picking almonds on the weekends and running the café at night."

"And now we get to go on our first date in Corfu."

I tilted my head at him. "I don't think this counts as a first date."

"No?"

"Friends with benefits don't get first dates."

"Ah." Seb pushed off the wall. "Let's go get food anyway, date or no. I'm starving."

It was a good thing it wasn't a first date; we ended up stopping at the first spanakopita cart we saw and eating our pies as we walked the streets again. Once our bellies were full and our fingers clean, we popped into shops.

Half the shops were selling specialty food items. Seb and I took turns sniffing herbs or tasting honey or olive oil. I bought a few items for fun experimentation, like candied kumquats and lemon preserves.

"Hey, smell this soap," I said as I turned around. Seb wasn't there; instead Malcom, the engineer who worked under Edie, was stepping into the shop.

"Hey, Marcella," he said, giving me an easy smile.

"Malcom, hey!" I said a little too loudly. "Doing some shopping?"

"Yeah, picking up gifts for my mum. How's the soap?"

"The what?" He nodded at the canary-yellow soap I'd forgotten was in my hand. "Oh, right. Olive oil and sea salt."

Malcom leaned in to sniff the bar just as Seb turned the corner of the aisle behind him. Our eyes widened at each other, and he ducked back behind the shelving.

"That's pretty good," Malcom said, and picked up a lavender soap bar.

I plopped mine back on the display. "All right, well, I'll see you back on the boat," I called over my shoulder as I escaped out of the shop. I turned left and walked a few meters down the road and waited. A few minutes later Seb came out, quickly swiveled his head to find me, and then trotted toward me, laughing.

"It's not funny." I poked his side, even though I was laughing too. "We almost got caught."

Seb pulled me under his arm. "Want to head back?"

"Sounds good. I've done enough damage for one day," I said, holding up my bag. "Besides, I think it might be best if we can disappear for a few hours where no one will catch us."

TWENTY-FIVE

We lay on the bed, breathing hard and letting the sweat cool off our skin. Seb's head was down by my hip, his breath blowing hot air over my flesh. His legs were crammed into the space by my shoulder on the inside of the bed, knees bent and legs akimbo. I slid an arm around one of his legs and let my fingers trail over his oblique muscles.

Seb propped his head up to look at me and grinned. "You look pretty fucking sexy all blissed out."

"Cocky," I teased, tugging at his leg hair. He grunted and rolled his upper body over me, pinning my arm between us and resting his head on my thigh. I sighed and closed my eyes, enjoying the way he stroked a light hand up my stomach.

Seb's head came off my thigh. "Who are those people?"

I opened my eyes and looked up, following his gaze to the framed photograph on the desk. "Those are my great-grandparents."

"Wow," he remarked. "They look fancy."

"They were fancy." I rested my head back down on the pillow, but Seb shifted and moved above me. He swung a leg over my head and straddled me backward. "What are you doing?" I said, mystified.

"Getting the photo."

"That view was . . ."

He looked over his shoulder and winked before throwing his other leg around and sliding off my bed. "You can have any view you want, flaquita."

With Seb's long arms, he didn't even have to take a step before picking up the frame. He climbed back on the mattress with me, sitting at the head of the bed. "Tell me about this."

"It's just a picture of my great-grandparents."

Seb looked up, serious, and nudged me. "Come on, Marce. I know what a pain it is to have personal things to truck around when we have our jobs. And yet you have this, so tell me about it."

I struggled up and sat next to Seb. "This is my great-grandpa Alfieri Giordano, and my great-grandma Tonia. And in this photo, they're on the *Monte Rosa,* a cruise ship, in 1931."

"Jesús." Seb squinted at the photo and looked closer. "I don't have any photographs of my great-grandparents. And this is . . . not just an old photo, but wow. A cruise ship in the 1930s . . ."

"Yeah, it's pretty neat."

"I wonder where they were going," Seb said.

"Norway."

He gaped at me. "How do you know that?"

"Nonna Tonia wrote a diary about the trip, and there was a whole photo album. I found it all up in our old, musty attic when I was a kid."

"That must have been amazing to read."

I shrugged. "It was a little tough to read, actually. I was at this age where I was starting to rebel against my parents, and reading the journal . . ."

Seb wrapped his arm around me, waiting patiently for me to go on.

"It was really obvious to me, even at my age, that my great-grandparents had had a lot of money. And money was something that was argued about constantly in my home growing up. We never had enough. And I pieced things together while I was a teenager that my dad had made some bad investments, sunk some money into the orchard my parents have, and the way the industry was turning . . . Anyway, my mom resented my dad a lot."

"Are they still together?"

"Yeah, amazingly enough. Visiting them is a major pain. It's all very loud, Italian, yelling, and not in the good way."

"I wondered why you flew straight from Tahiti to here. It would have been a good chance to stop in at home if you'd wanted to."

"No, thanks." I shuddered. "What about you?"

"My family?"

I nodded.

Seb put the frame down on the bed and sighed. "My parents live in Miami, if you remember?"

"Yes, they're from Cuba."

"Yeah. It was not easy for them to immigrate, and we had a pretty tough life for a while. I was born in the States, though, so I was too young to remember most of it."

"Are you close to them now?"

"Not really." Seb pulled me tighter into his chest. "They hate my career path and wanted me to keep doing minimum-wage restaurant work like they did. They were always pushing me to work hard, like it was only hard work you needed, not education or luck or passion."

"How did you end up working on yachts, then?"

"Have you been to Miami?"

I shook my head.

"It's just chock-full of superyachts. Like Nice and Monaco. And I always saw the crews on board, guys like me, young Latinos, and thought it was amazing that they could live on a boat like that as their jobs. And everyone knew who owned the boats—old white dudes. To me, it just seemed like this is how I could move up in life."

"Wow. That's exactly how I feel. Like, my great-grandparents were off on these big cruise ship adventures, hugely ahead of their time. And this is the best way that I felt I could do it."

Seb rubbed my back and yawned.

"We've had a long, fun day."

"Yeah, we have," Seb replied, sleep tinting his voice. "I liked spending the day with you, Marce."

"I liked it too."

He squeezed my shoulders. "I like *you*."

TWENTY-SIX

After nearly a week of projects, Dom declared us fit to leave, and with favorable weather, we departed for Malta. It would take us eighteen hours to make the passage from Corfu, but instead of doing the passage during the day, we would do it at night.

Roy and I had prepared food for the crew to reheat and snacks to grab quickly throughout the passage. The less time we spent in the galley while underway, the less potential for accidents and seasickness.

Seb slipped into my room that night. My bunk rocked gently with *Themis*'s movements, and our quiet kisses in the dark turned frantic quickly.

"Damn it," Seb said, pulling back. "I forgot the condoms in my cabin. I'll be right back."

"Wait, Seb." I grabbed at his arm before he could step away from the bed. "I am on birth control."

Seb froze.

"And I've been tested and I'm clean. I haven't been with anyone since you."

"I'd rather just use a condom, if you don't mind." Seb looked wary, so I smiled and shooed him away.

"Get one, then, and come back to bed."

His face relaxing, Seb threw on shorts and disappeared out the door, returning a few minutes later with the condom. He ripped open the wrapper and rolled it on before climbing up in bed behind me. "On your stomach." He patted my hip.

I twisted over and spread my legs wide. I could always feel Seb's eyes on us, watching himself pump in and out, and I enjoyed the way it riled him up.

He thrusted into me, making sure we were both slick before he sat up on his heels. Both palms gripped my cheeks firmly and his thumbs slid down the crease between my butt and thighs. Seb rocked slowly, almost carefully, in and out, shallow strokes designed to tease while he watched. I gave as good as I got, rotating my hips and adding a twist to our movements. I could barely see him out of the corner of my eye, but his panting breath and his firm grip made me clench around him quickly.

Seb couldn't keep it slow for very long, and his

control fell apart. He bent over me, pushing my hips down and blowing hot breath on the back of my neck. Everything was needy and urgent, peaking in erratic movements until he came with a shout.

He rolled, his weight shifting off my back and dipping the bed beside me. We caught our breath together.

I turned to my side as Seb relaxed beside me. His arm was thrown over his forehead, his other hand resting on his chest. I traced a finger up to his throat, smoothing some of the hairs I found there with my fingertip. He swallowed, his Adam's apple bobbing underneath me. I waited patiently, trying to give him time to recover without letting the moment pass.

"Seb." I waited for him to look at me. "Should we go get tested together? Would that make you more comfortable?"

Perhaps I didn't wait long enough; Seb sat up, swinging his legs over the side of the bed, and stalked off to the head to take care of the condom and cleanup. When he returned, he put his face in his hands and sighed before turning toward me. He placed his palms on the bed, pressing the mattress down, then gently pulled me toward him.

"It's not that." He stopped, and I patiently waited while he gathered his thoughts.

"When I was seventeen, my girlfriend of two years got pregnant."

Oh shit. I sat up next to Seb, placing my hand on his arm. I stayed quiet, letting him go at his own pace.

"I'd already been working around the marina and I'd just been offered a job, a weeklong charter trip to the Bahamas. I was so sure I was going to get out. Of my parents' restaurant, of our hood, of Miami. But everything crashed down. My parents were thrilled, for a lot of reasons; they wanted me to stay, they wanted a daughter, they wanted something to bind them even tighter to America. And of course, I didn't want to be a deadbeat dad, so I passed on the job and proposed."

He paused, the pain of his own story eating him up. "Then I found out that my girlfriend had cheated, and the baby was probably the other guy's. I wanted nothing to do with her, but my parents begged me to go through with it, to marry a cheater and to raise a kid who wasn't mine."

This time Seb was quiet for longer, until I gently prompted him. "What happened?"

"She did the test, it wasn't mine, and my parents were heartbroken. I just wanted to get the hell out of Miami, so I took the first job I could find to take me offshore. That was six years ago." He turned to look me in the eye and said quietly, "I didn't want to give up my dream then, and I won't give my dream up now. You have to be really sure you understand that."

"I know. I know that birth control isn't one hundred percent effective, but I understand your concerns. I don't want a child either."

"So where does that leave us?"

I wrapped my arms around his waist from behind, kissing his shoulder. "We keep using condoms."

Seb's arm slid over mine and he glanced back at me. "You don't mind?"

"No. It's way more important that you are comfortable than anything else."

He tipped his forehead against mine, closing his eyes briefly. "Thanks."

"I'm sorry about your family," I told him quietly.

"Me too. I was, and still am, so angry at my parents. But it's been a few years, and sometimes I'm just *homesick,* you know? It's not just my parents, either; it's Miami, the community, the food, Little Havana." He paused, deep in his memories. "Sometimes I want to go home, even just to visit, but I feel that if I go home before really making my career happen, then I'll come home a failure, and my parents will tell me I should have just worked harder."

I squeezed his hand and tugged him back down onto the bed. "You are definitely not a failure."

Seb curled into my side, resting his head on my shoulder. "Thanks, Marce."

I played with his curls, letting my fingers tug and release the strands while I stared up at the ceiling. Seb's yearning for his family and his culture wasn't something I really understood, but on a deep level, I was jealous. He deserved a family who loved him, but how dare they try to keep him pinned down somewhere he didn't belong, where he would never become a captain and never would have met me.

Seb was nine years younger than me. It surprised me, but I suspected that his experience affected him beyond being careful with condoms. Having that weight of responsibility—not just of a child, but of holding on to who he was and what he wanted—that aged him too.

He'd given me a stronger glimpse of who he was: behind the easy smiles and the flirting, Seb was still trying to find his place, just like me. My heart beat hard in my chest as he shifted against my shoulder.

For the first time, I wished I could give him that place.

TWENTY-SEVEN

THEMIS WAS ANCHORED STERN-TO TO THE WHARF IN THE Grand Harbour of Malta. The stern gangway was down, and our view to the aft was directly out at the stone walls of Fort St. Angelo. To either side, including the view outside my galley window, were more superyachts. Since we'd arrived, one of the first ones on the scene, the harbor had filled with other boats, and walking down the dock was a flurry of activity as crews cleaned and polished their boats, getting prepared for their owners' arrival.

I barely noticed. Instead Roy and I had been swamped with deliveries and prep work. Natasha, Justin, and Alex would arrive tonight, and the regatta would start tomorrow. We would have a full day motoring around as a spectator boat, and then we would spend the next day dockside, preparing for the evening's awards ceremony on *Themis* at the dock.

The checklist in my hands was nearly complete. I flipped back and forth, comparing notes with the delivery slip and with my order. Substitutions had been made, and I was not happy about it.

"This isn't the Imperia we ordered." I pointed at the box of caviar.

"Right, this is just as good, but cheaper."

I stared at the delivery guy. "Do we look like we give a shit if it's cheaper? Send it back, and get me the proper product by noon; otherwise, I'll order from my other vendor."

Returning to the list, I confirmed a few more items. "Radicchios instead of endives?"

This time he stubbornly shook his head. "There's a shortage of those. No one else has them either."

I regarded him skeptically. "Fine, I'll accept this substitution, but I'm going to ask around."

Another truck pulled up at the stern. "Will!" I shouted toward the bar. "Your champagne is here!"

"Thanks!" came the call back.

I eyed a guy walking up to us wearing a chef's jacket, but he stood to the side waiting his turn. I quickly went through the rest of the list and made some notes on what I still needed to track down. The delivery guy scuttled off and I turned my attention to the chef.

"Can I help you?" The guy was tall and lean, with olive skin like mine and stubble over his face.

He smiled and offered his hand, speaking to me in beautiful Italian. "Marcella? I'm Andre. We've been emailing?"

"Oh yes, hello." I shook his offered hand. "You're on *Pegasus,* right? Which one is she?"

He pointed over his shoulder. "Three boats down, the power yacht with the Cayman Islands flag."

"Beautiful. I'm really glad to have your team coming to help for the weekend." Andre and some of the stews were coming aboard *Themis* to help out our staff. Andre was a head chef, like me, and he'd be assisting in the galley alongside Roy. The owners of *Pegasus,* the Kozlovas, were friends of Natasha and Justin's. Their kids would race together in the regatta over the weekend.

"Come on aboard. I'll give you the tour and we can go over the menu."

HALF AN HOUR LATER WE SAT IN THE CREW LOUNGE, going over the game plan. Andre had been wide-eyed as we toured the service stations around *Themis,* but as soon as we were in the galley, he was all business. With a crowd of a hundred people, the biggest issue would usually be dealing with the dirty dishes, so Andre's team was going to come in handy washing dishes and serving. Andre would focus on the displays, keeping them full, and some of the simpler hors d'oeuvres.

Since Natasha and Justin were so particular, I would handle the majority of the assemblage, but Andre's team would spend the day of the regatta prepping food—dicing, slicing, mincing, searing, anything I needed done in advance—on *Pegasus.*

It was a pleasure to talk to Andre in my native tongue, and when we wrapped up the list of prep work, we compared notes from home. "I'm from Rome," he told me. "And I studied in Italy, but I understand you went to school in London?"

"Yes, my menus have gotten much more international, which is good for this job, since the Boyds are Brits."

"Have you heard about the kids?"

I closed my portfolio. "What kids?"

"I guess they aren't kids anymore, but Alex Boyd and Niki Kozlova got into some drama on Instagram." He raised his eyebrows and shrugged. "Alex and Niki were friends in school, and that's how the parents met. But . . . teenagers." He shrugged.

"Somewhere along the way hormones kicked in and now they are absolute nemeses. They started showing up at events just to antagonize each other: polo, charity balls, sailing races. But then they ended up on the same boat together for a regatta in Bermuda, and all hell broke loose."

Over Andre's shoulder, I saw Roy come into the galley with a box of greens and nod at us.

"They will both be on the same yacht in the regatta this weekend?" I asked.

"No, thank God. They are too competitive. But they'll both be at the awards ceremony that night."

I frowned. "They don't get disruptive, do they?"

"Not that I've seen. Just passive-aggressive postings on social media and occasionally harmless pranks. I've only met the Boyds a few times, but the Kozlovas keep Niki in check pretty well." He leaned his elbows on the table. "How long have you been on *Themis*?"

"I've been here six weeks."

"Is it going well? I've heard Natasha's tough to work for. When the Kozlovas are really trying to impress her, they hire a famous chef." He raised his hands. "I'm good, but not that good. You must be quite talented."

I inclined my head. "Thank you. It has been okay so far. We had a horrible charter." I told Andre about the ridiculous guests and the mayhem on board. He winced in sympathy and patted my hand, lingering a little bit on my skin, making the hairs on the back of my neck stand up in warning. I glanced over at Roy, who met my eyes. His brow furrowed and he glanced at my hand.

Andre pulled my attention back to him. "Well, as close as the Boyds and Kozlovas are, we might bump into each other quite a bit. I hear *Themis* is heading to the Caribbean next season too."

I pulled my hand out from under his and gathered up my things. "It certainly seems like it. Let's hope this weekend goes well; otherwise, you may never see me again." I laughed weakly.

"Nonsense, we will triumph." He shook my hand and nodded to Roy. "I'll see myself out. Marcella, it was a pleasure." He turned and switched back to English. "Bye."

No sooner had the door closed than Roy turned to me. "Who is that?"

I tied an apron on. "That is Andre from *Pegasus,* a few boats down. He and his crew are being lent to us for the weekend, remember?"

Roy made a face. "That guy? He's a tosser."

I leaned a hip against the counter and crossed my arms. "How would you know? He barely said two words in English while you were here."

"Honey, I don't need to speak the language to identify a moron. Seb is going to *hate* that guy."

I blew out a frustrated breath. This was part of my job, and for the regatta, I couldn't afford to turn down help. "It doesn't matter. It's just one night, and we'll power through and get the work done. We need this crew to help."

"Just make sure he speaks English while he's here," Roy grumbled.

We worked through the rest of the evening, interrupted only once as the Boyds returned from dinner out with their newly arrived son.

"Knock, knock," a posh British voice called from the stairwell. A young man stood in the doorway, a near spitting image of Natasha, but taller than even Justin.

Roy looked up from dicing and broke into a grin. "Alex! Good to see you, man." He wiped his hands on his towel then offered Justin and Natasha's son a handshake.

"Good to see you too." Alex turned to me. "You must be Marcella." He held out his hand.

"Nice to meet you, Alex."

"Pleasure. Hopefully Roy's been good to you since you've joined us?"

"Absolutely." I leaned a hip against the counter.

"Good. I just wanted to pop in and say hello. I

know it's a hellish day for you both, and I won't be around much anyway the next few days."

"Yeah, mate, good luck in the regatta tomorrow. I placed my bets, so I've got some money riding on you and a few chore swaps on the line too."

Alex laughed. "If I lose, who are you going to have to cook for?"

"Breakfast in bed for Xavier."

"Thanks, Roy. I'll be sure to think about your dignity while I'm blowing over the finish line."

TWENTY-EIGHT

THE FIRST DAY OF THE REGATTA WAS INTENSE. WE HAD fifty guests aboard, and the crew filtered in and out of the galley constantly. Roy and I worked all day as the stews called out for whatever they needed: refills for the crudité station, one of the children running around had dunked their entire hand in the yogurt bowl and then in the strawberry bowl and we had to replace them both for cross-contamination, and where the hell had the basil gotten to?

Just like with their favorite breakfast, Natasha and Justin seemed thrilled with the simplicity and classic presentation we gave. The food all came out amazing—I personally checked every dish myself, coming up to the main deck for observation runs—but it was simple and hearty.

I walked up the stairs to do another run-through

and check the displays myself. I was carrying a bowl of oranges up for Will at the bar, and as soon as I set the bowl down, Natasha called my name.

"Marcella, so glad to see you up here enjoying the day. Do you have a moment?" She steered me by my elbow toward a couple standing by the rail. One thing I'd learned about boaters was that what could appear to be dressed-down was very much not. The main deck was full of people wearing Bermuda shorts and loafers, sundresses and sandals. All very casual-looking, until you spotted the logos of H/H and Henri Lloyd.

She introduced me to some friends of hers, and then we moved on to another group and another. I resisted checking my watch, reminding myself that Roy was capable.

"Which boat is Alex's?" I asked Natasha in a lull in conversation, stepping up to the rail and shielding my eyes from the sun. We were outside the harbor, looking at the island of Malta, which was several miles off. In the distance, I could see dozens of smaller sailboats, their multicolored spinnakers flying in the light breeze as they approached us.

"His spinnaker is the light blue one. With the Boyd Technologies logo, naturally."

From this far away, I could tell which one was the light blue one, but the logo of Natasha's company was too hard to make out. She handed me a pair of binoculars and I was able to see it better.

"How many people are on each boat?"

"Only two. Alex and his best friend, Daniel."

I put the binoculars down and turned to Natasha. "How is he doing in the race?"

She couldn't hide the pride in her voice, her eyes still staying trained on the sails. "It's too soon to call anything, but so far they're in the lead."

"Lovely." I glanced around the deck, at the food stations, which were still voluptuous, and the wait-staff darting back and forth with cocktails. "If everything is to your satisfaction up here, I will need to go back down to the galley."

Natasha waved me off. "Yes, wonderful. Please do what you need to do."

As I turned away, Seb caught my eye, standing watch from the starboard side of *Themis*. He winked at me, and I hid my smile as I stepped back inside.

"Good evening." The words in Italian startled me, and I nearly dropped the pastry bag I was washing. Andre stood at the corner of the room, a smile on his face. "One of your crew said I could come in." We were back on the dock in Grand Harbour. It was late:

the Boyds had already returned from dinner out and most of the crew had gone off to sleep early, preparing for a big day tomorrow.

I was alone in the galley, having sent Roy off to bed early. He would wake in the morning to prepare breakfast for the crew. Natasha and Justin were having brunch out with the owners of *Pegasus,* so while I was free from making breakfast, I was going to be spending the whole day preparing for the evening's party. I had just wanted to test out the consistency for one of the cheese fillings for tomorrow before I went to bed. Natasha wanted more tartness in it, so I was sampling and testing with more lemons.

"Yes, of course. How was the day on *Pegasus*? Good?"

"It was. We were out by one of the other turns, but I could see *Themis* from my window. Could you see us?"

I grimaced. "Too busy to notice, unfortunately."

"Ah. Well, we had fewer people on *Pegasus*. The Kozlovas don't enjoy strangers on their boat. Besides, everyone wants to be on the magical *Themis*."

"I think they kept the number pretty low," I said. "Exclusivity and whatnot."

Andre moved to lean his hip against the counter next to me. He crossed his arms and smiled.

I dunked the pastry bag under the water again. "Did you need something?"

"I had a few last-minute suggestions for tomorrow's menu, if you are interested."

I raised an eyebrow. This was *my* galley, *my* big event. Which started tomorrow. What exactly was he trying to change? "Oh? Natasha has personally approved and tasted a lot of the menu items; I doubt there's going to be much that I'm willing to change."

Andre spread his hands out in front of him. "Humor me, please. I'd like to get your opinion on some of the ideas I have had."

I glanced at the clock. My alarm would go off in six hours to wake me up.

"All right, but let's make it quick."

"All work and no play on *Themis,* huh?" Andre called over his shoulder as he retreated to the crew lounge and pulled out some papers. I finished drying the pastry bag and prayed that he would be quick.

I wanted to stay standing and try to keep this short, but I was too tired on my feet. I slid into the booth next to Andre and looked over the notes. "Natasha doesn't like nasturtium," I mumbled, and crossed out the plating suggestion. Some of the ideas were ones I'd already run past Natasha but she had vetoed them. The rest just wouldn't work.

I didn't mean to be harsh, but I was tired and not

even close to being done. "Andre, these won't work." I tossed the papers down and started to stand up. Instead Andre's hand gripped my shoulder, pulling me back down and a little closer to him.

"Now, hold on, Marcella. These ideas are good. If your boss wasn't so uptight, these would be perfect for the event."

My heart started to pound, and I tried to wiggle out from under his hand. "Andre—"

He cut me off. "It seems like Natasha's bitchiness is rubbing off on you." He pulled me in tighter. "You could put in a good word for me. You need me to pull off this event."

I gritted my teeth. His grip tightened, his fingers digging into my skin. I'd dealt with misogyny and sexism in the workplace, but for the first time, it seemed like someone was willing to hurt me. "Let me go."

And just like I'd said the magic words, Seb appeared in the doorway. He stepped menacingly into the room. "Get. Out." His jaw was tense, his eyes angry.

Andre's hand lifted off my shoulder, the corner of his mouth ticking down in a slight frown. I slid away from him, standing up and slinking across the room. Andre's eyes were calculating and my heart sunk. Seb was just guessing, running off instinct when he didn't even know the language. "Hey, man," Andre said in English, clocking Seb's American accent. "We were just talking about tomorrow's menu."

Seb's eyes narrowed. "We know exactly what you were talking about, Andre. Get. Out." He shifted, revealing Gio standing right behind him.

"Vaffanculo," Gio bit out.

Andre set his jaw and rose to his feet. "How do you think Natasha is going to take this, eh? There's no way your team can pull off the event tomorrow alone. It'll be a disgrace to *Themis.* You *need* my help."

"No we don't," Seb ground out.

"Fine. I'll tell the Kozlovas that you don't need me." Andre held his hands up. "If you think you can do so well without me, with your," he gestured at me and Seb stepped threateningly toward him, "new chef, turn down my help. I have years of experience on yachts with events like this. If you think you can do this on your own, fine."

The blood drained from my face. He was right: my job hung on a precarious balance, and refusing Andre's help would certainly tip it over.

He tossed a look back at me. "Maybe if you beg."

Fortunately, Gio shoved Seb aside before he could do something dumb like punch Andre. They stepped out of the way and Gio followed Andre up to escort him off the boat.

Seb turned his gaze to me, running up and down my body. "Are you okay?"

"Yes." I took a big inhale and breathed out, trying to quell the sense of panic. How were we going to pull off the party when suddenly I had twice as much work to do? I had been counting on the staff on *Pegasus* to keep doing prep work tomorrow, to help with washing dishes and use of their ovens. I blinked away my terror. "How did you even overhear us? Shouldn't you be in bed?"

Seb threw a glance at the doorway and stepped toward me. One hand grasped mine, and the other came up to gently touch my cheek. "Roy mentioned that guy earlier, and seemed worried about him. I couldn't sleep, so I wandered over, and when I heard you talking in Italian . . . I didn't want to make a big deal out of nothing, and I knew Gio was doing the late-night rounds, so I asked him to eavesdrop."

"Wow." My heart wasn't calming down. Yes, in some sense I had been lucky for Seb's hunch, but at what cost?

He chuckled. "Yeah, pretty lucky, right?"

"Lucky?" I said incredulously. "How was losing half our kitchen staff for tomorrow lucky?" All the anger Andre had stirred up suddenly had a new target.

Seb's face fell, and his eyes lit with anger. "That's

what you are going to worry about, Marce?" His jaw tensed in the moment suspended between us. Then he continued, his voice low. "I will *never* let you sacrifice your safety for your job."

We were interrupted by Gio coming back down the stairs, Dom on his heels. Seb dropped contact with me, and I recounted the story to Dom, who assured me he'd talk it over with Natasha and Justin.

"What, exactly, do we do now?" I said, throttling to keep the panic out of my voice. "Andre's going to blame us, say we refused his help and wash his hands of this. Even if we wanted his help, it's going to be a huge mess. I have to assume that I'm on my own for tomorrow."

Seb let out a deep breath next to me, pinching the bridge of his nose. "Goddamn it."

"You aren't on your own." Dom placed a hand on my shoulder, firm and strong. "You've got all the crew with you, okay? This is important to Natasha, and it's important to all of us. Go get some sleep, and we'll talk in the morning."

Seb trailed behind me as I walked through to my cabin. When we arrived at my door, he shoved his hands into his pockets and searched my face. "Do you want me to stay?"

"No."

Seb let my response hang for a moment. "Are you going to be able to sleep?"

I snapped. "I'm not a child, Seb. You don't need to hover and fix everything for me."

"Whoa, whoa. Marcella, I know this isn't ideal—"

"It's not ideal?" I sneered at him.

"Hey, I'm not the one who put your job on the line. That was him." He pointed an aggressive finger down the hall. "Don't be angry at me."

"I lost half my crew for tomorrow." To my horror, tears stung my eyes. I was losing control in a way that had never happened before. Kitchens were a pressure cooker, and even by myself, in the little galley on this ship, I was imploding.

"Marce," Seb said gently. "He would have done something else. Maybe sabotaged something tomorrow or taken advantage of you when everyone else was busy." He swept a hand up my arm and onto my shoulder. "It's your name on the event. Anything that could happen would just end up being a he-said, she-said nightmare. You are better off without him, and you can do it. I know it."

I took a few deep breaths. Perhaps Seb was right and it was better to have this guy out the night before instead of in the heat of activity the day of. I blinked hard, feeling myself deflate.

"Yeah, okay." I shook my arms out. "Sleep now, problem-solve tomorrow."

"Okay. I know I'm being overly cautious, but let me hear you lock your door."

I stepped in and turned around to close the door behind me. When the door was just a crack open, I paused. "Thank you, Seb."

"Good night, Marcella."

TWENTY-NINE

I WOKE EARLY, DRESSED IN MY UNIFORM, AND GAVE myself a pep talk. A very terrible pep talk. "Let's do the best we can. We will not get fired today, Marcella."

The main deck was bustling with activity already, and a young woman who I didn't recognize was pushing a cart full of food off the boat and down the gangway.

"Hey, wait!" I reached out a hand and the woman turned. She was dressed in uniform, but instead of *Pegasus* on the logo like I was expecting, it read *Lady Elmira*. My brain stuttered for a moment. "Wait, who are you? Where is all this food going?"

"Marcella!" Roy called out behind me. He stopped beside me. "Go ahead, Annette. Thanks." He nodded at her and she pushed the cart again.

"What's going on?"

"Dom can probably explain it better, but he's busy right now. Andre is gone—I don't know, and I didn't ask," Roy said when he saw my face. "But the rest of *Pegasus*'s crew is still coming to help us out today. The food, though"—he gestured and pulled us aside as someone came up the gangway with a cart of dinnerware—"the food is going next door. Thankfully, we were able to recruit—well, I say recruit but in actuality it was more like Natasha forcefully bribed—the chef to prep in his kitchen for the day instead." Roy winced. "We can't get everything done, but it'll be a lot."

"Wow, this is . . . unexpected."

Roy laughed. "It was very impressive to see. Natasha is a bit of a dervish when she's been slighted. It helps that Dom knows the bosun next door pretty well." He shrugged. "Small world, right?"

I turned around, surveying all the effort being done to pull this event off, not just from the food side, but every way possible. The boat swarmed with staff who polished and cleaned. I stood, blinking in amazement, and let a glimmer of hope sweep over me for a moment before I snapped myself out of it.

Time to get to work.

THROUGHOUT THE DAY, I SENT OFF FOOD NEXT DOOR. Whole produce that went over with instructions like "dice" or "chiffon" came back perfectly done. It was like having my own row of invisible interns all day long.

Cat had barely been in the galley all day, and I hoped that everything was going well for her team. The stews came and went, following their own instructions and operating independently from me and Roy.

High-heeled steps clacked down the stairwell as I finished the last swirls of a tempered chocolate and placed them in the fridge to chill. Natasha was beside me as I closed the door.

"Marcella, how are you today?" Her eyes scrutinized me. I glanced at the clock; I hadn't been expecting her back on board for at least another half hour. My chef's jacket was spotted, my apron a little lopsided, and wisps of hair stuck to my forehead.

"Things are going well." It wasn't a lie; we *were* a little behind, but given the circumstances, it could have been worse.

"I know you don't have much time to chat, but I wanted to assure you that I take slights against my crew seriously." She cocked her head. "Restaurants are a competitive male-dominated industry, so I imagine it's not unlike technology when I got into the game. Whilst the event tonight is important, I would be a fool to overlook my long-term goals."

"Thank you?"

"That doesn't mean I don't have my usual expectations, though. Don't let me down."

"Yes, ma'am."

I swear she clicked her heels. "Right. Carry on. I look forward to the service tonight."

Roy chuckled at the counter opposite me. "Warm and fuzzy, that one, but she's got your back."

Two minutes later the door opened again and this time it was Cat who stepped into the galley. "Half past, Marce. Let's do a walk-through so you can answer a few questions and then I can leave you in peace." I ditched my apron, traded my jacket in for a clean one, and followed Cat up the stairs.

The main deck had been completely transformed. Potted plants were scattered throughout, with uplighting and drapery that tastefully hid the backbones of the temporary structures. Waitstaff in smart uniforms scuttled here and there. Will, in a bow tie and vest, was shaking cocktails, and his assistant, who I'd never seen before but was similarly dressed, poured champagne into tulip glasses.

We passed around the bar into the atrium. I came

to a sudden stop; Seb was passing in the opposite direction. He was dressed in a tux, with an earpiece and a name badge. His hair was swept back and styled, his beard neatly trimmed.

He grinned at me and adjusted his sleeve. "Hey, Marce."

"Hi." Cat continued on without me and I heard her talking to someone in the dining room. I looked Seb up and down. "You clean up nice."

"Thanks. Working usher-slash-security today, making sure all the drunk partygoers get their photos up at the helm and don't accidentally press buttons they shouldn't be touching."

"You'll be up on the bridge deck, then?"

He nodded. "All night. I suspect you'll be equally busy downstairs tonight, eh?" He leaned in closer. "Who do you think is going to get off first tonight?"

My stomach fluttered. "I think we'll both be exhausted."

Seb leaned away, tucking his hands into his pockets. "We may be exhausted tonight, but we all have tomorrow off, and there's no place I'd rather wake up than next to you."

Heat crept up my body, and I eyed the door nervously, hoping Cat was occupied enough not to overhear.

A glint in his eye, Seb leaned in again. "Naked, sleepy morning sex sounds perfect after a hard day's work."

"Hush." I pushed him gently away. "Let's just play it by ear. There's a lot going on, and I really need to get back downstairs."

"All right." He glanced around and, finding us still alone, leaned down and kissed my cheek. "Good luck tonight."

Then he and his tuxedoed glory were gone.

THE EVENING WAS A BLUR, ROY AND I A FLURRY OF activity. The stews came and went, gossiping and gasping over guest antics, though this was a fairly tame event and we didn't have anyone throwing up overboard or otherwise creating drama.

"The security guys have had to block nonstop. People think they can just get dressed up and waltz on board any boat," I overheard Bok say.

Roy chimed in without looking up from the dish he was plating. "The sous chef on *Lady Elmira* told me the rejects are trying to get on their boat instead. They—and some other boats down the dock—have pulled up their gangways to discourage crashers."

The oven door slammed closed behind me as I pulled a tray of puff pastry Wellington bites out. "How is it going upstairs?"

"Good," Bok assured me. "Natasha has a very pleasant, giggly buzz."

I raised an eyebrow.

"I know," she said. "I didn't realize she had that setting, but yes, it's true."

Roy was arranging plates on Bok's tray when the radio crackled in our ears. "Um, Cat," Xavier interrupted, "we've got a situation upstairs with the dessert display. Better get Marcella, too."

There was a tiny pause in activity in the room, and Roy and I exchanged a concerned glance. I switched my radio on. "Marcella here, on my way."

Walking quickly up the crew stairs and toward the bow of the boat, Cat fell into step beside me. When we rounded the corner, we were met with the security team shooing guests aft, away from the shouting match on deck.

"You just can't accept that I won." Alex stood on the deck, towering over a petite waif of a young woman. He was shrugging off his suit, which hung oddly off his shoulders. As one arm came out, the back of the jacket twisted, revealing a smashed collection of creams and fondant crusted onto the fabric.

"It was an accident!" the young woman across from him shrieked. "And I could stand it just fine if you'd stopped rubbing your win in my face. Sailing was *my* thing and you've got your spindly, grubby hands all over it."

The dessert table had been overturned, and several staff members were already at work cleaning up around the fighting couple. I spun to face Cat, but she was gone.

"And I'm better at it than you. Maybe if you spent more time with your sailing coach instead of that shitty boyfriend of yours, you might have done better," he hissed. They were toe-to-toe now, teeth clenched and bare feet grinding the pastries down into the deck.

"Fuck. Off. Alex."

"Niki!" came a sharp voice from behind me. "What is the meaning of this? Stop this nonsense right now!" An elegant platinum blonde, presumably Niki's mother, stepped out onto the deck, Cat behind her. "Seriously, I don't know what has gotten into you two."

Natasha appeared from the other side. Her voice matched her gaze: disappointed. "Alex, obviously, we've let this feud between you two go on long enough. The award part is over, and dessert looks like it'll be delayed, thanks to you two. Apologize to the staff and go down to your room."

Alex bowed his head to the two women. "My apologies, Mum, Ana." He tipped his head to me as well. "Sorry, Marcella." He glanced around the deck and was gone.

"You're going back to *Pegasus* too. This is far too much disappointment for one weekend." The mother tugged her daughter in front of Natasha.

"Sorry, Mrs. Boyd." Niki looked down at her feet.

Natasha rolled her eyes. "I can't believe you two are twenty-four years old and we have to send you to your rooms like children."

Niki stalked off down the deck.

"I'm terribly sorry, Nat," Ana offered.

Natasha waved it off. "Marcella, do we have replacements downstairs?"

"Yes, ma'am, we'll work on plating up new trays."

"I'll get the display table fixed up again," said Cat as she and Bok worked to right the table.

"Thank you, both. Now, Ana, we've got to sort out these two kids of ours. . . ." She hooked her arm through Ana's and led her aft. "Did you know Alex has a charity fundraiser next month in New York City? I think Niki should be there too."

I followed the two women out and diverted to the staff area while trying to ignore their conversation; they lamented Niki's boyfriend, pined for grandkids, and were clearly planning to meddle in their children's lives.

But then again, Seb looked at me the same way Alex had looked at Niki.

We reset the table, and working double time on the desserts put us behind washing the dishes. It was late, very late, when Seb strolled into the galley, finished with his responsibilities. Without a word, he stripped off his coat and rolled up his sleeves. We worked quietly, everyone dragging in exhaustion from the evening's work.

Cat set down a tray of miscellaneous bar supplies. "That's the last of Will's. The main deck is closed up. Marcella, are you good in here?"

"Yes, tell all your stews thank you for a job well done."

She came up behind me and curled her arms around my shoulders, resting her chin to the left. "You did a great job today." She squeezed harder. "Honestly, it could have been a clusterfuck, but you were phenomenal."

She squeezed me and my chest swelled. Glancing up, Roy caught my eye and grinned. Suddenly I didn't feel so tired.

I leaned my head against Cat's. "Thanks. Go get some sleep."

She let me go and the stews filtered out, calling good nights and see you tomorrows.

It was just me, Roy, and Seb in the galley now. Roy glanced at me, then spun around to look at Seb.

"Seriously?" he scoffed at us both. "Get out."

"What? No, we're almost done."

"It's fine, Marce. Get to bed. I'll handle it from here. There's not much left to do and I know you've earned a treat." He smirked at me.

Seb shut the sanitizer firmly and reached back to untie his apron. "I'm on board."

"Roy, I'm your boss."

"Don't care."

Seb tossed his apron into the laundry and stood behind me, untying mine. I should argue more, I knew, but it just wasn't in me. I was tired, and now that the event was officially over, I was draining by the minute.

"Come on," Seb coaxed. "You'll still have plenty to do in the morning."

"Thanks, Roy," I called over my shoulder as Seb pushed me out of the galley and toward my cabin. "Dom is probably still awake," I warned Seb.

Seb snorted. "I think he's asleep up in the wheelhouse. Don't worry about Dom. I'm going to go shower in my room. I'll be back soon."

I nodded and made my way back to my room, where I stripped and stood under the showerhead for no more than thirty seconds, toweled off, and collapsed into bed.

THIRTY

It was late. My internal clock had hit snooze so many times, and when I woke up, I could tell it was well past sunrise. Seb's arm was thrown over my middle, and he was curled up on my side, his nose nuzzled into the spot just below my ear. His breath ghosted across my cheek.

"Morning," Seb said softly. Just hearing those raspy words, feeling the weight of Seb against my body, made my heart sing.

I stretched and twisted under the sheet, squeezing my eyes tight against the daylight that crept in around the window shades. "Good morning." I relaxed against the bed and Seb's warm hand slid up my back. He kneaded the muscles just under my shoulder blades, pressing firm fingers into the knots that had developed after bending over the counter all day yesterday. I groaned and squirmed.

Seb stilled. "Did that hurt?"

"Hurt so good," I mumbled. He huffed a laugh and kept massaging.

His fingers worked their way down, kneading firmly over my ass. Seb pressed closer to me, kissing my shoulder and twining a leg around mine, tugging me gently. His fingers slipped in between my legs, tracing over me. His kisses traveled across my back, until he shifted up on his elbow to lean farther over.

The pressure and warmth radiating from him worked together with his fingers, and I was soon slick and squirming. "Seb," I complained.

The weight of him pressed me down into the mattress as he slid on top of me. His chest covered my back, and he tucked his arms around my torso, twisting our fingers together under my chest. He nibbled my ear, and his hips flexed against me.

I leaned back, feeling his cock slot between my cheeks and his length press against my tailbone. When I turned my head a little bit farther, Seb met me for a kiss. His hips kept rocking, his fingers tight in mine.

On a gasp he pulled back. "Goddamn it. I'm going to get a condom."

"Hurry."

I turned my head the other way to watch him slip the condom on and climb back up onto the bed. He tucked his arms under me again and carefully worked his way inside me.

When he was fully seated, his hip bones against my butt, we both stilled. His breath tickled my ear, and I squeezed my thighs together, making him groan.

He rocked, slow and steady. I closed my eyes, feeling the slide and pull of him inside me, the weight of his body, the way he gripped my fingers so tight. In and out. Over and over.

He started chanting my name. "Marcella, Dios mío, Marcella."

"Seb." I let go of his hand, and he pushed up a little bit, giving me some space to get my fingers exactly where they needed to be. "Back down."

He grinned and complied, resting his weight on me again, his hand going to my shoulder now. He didn't move, just let me work on myself, dropping soft kisses down my neck and back while my body grew tighter and tighter.

Finally I gasped and pulsed around him, coming hard against my own hand.

Seb lightly bit my shoulder and grunted against my skin. He eased back, whispering, "Fuck, Marcella, that was so hot. . . ."

He picked up the pace, grinding down, chasing his own orgasm, when someone knocked on the door.

Seb froze.

The knock happened again, and to my horror, a voice called out from the other side. "Marcella?"

It was Justin. *Shit, shit, shit, shit.* I shoved Seb off me and he grunted. "Easy . . ."

"Shh." I put my finger to my lips in an urgent motion. "Seb, you have to hide."

His lips tipped up into a smile and he chuckled before he saw my face. "What, you're serious?"

"Seb, shut up and hide," I said through gritted teeth. "Get in the wardrobe, get into the head, I don't care, but hide."

Justin knocked again. "Marcella, sorry to bother you."

"Just a minute!" I called. I quickly threw on my clothes and Seb was not. Moving. Fast. Enough.

I grabbed an arm and dragged him out of the bed. He stumbled and bent to pick up a handful of clothes from the floor. I threw open the wardrobe—it was closer, and honestly, that was all I cared about.

I shoved Seb in and closed the door, smoothed my hair back, and took a deep breath.

"Mr. Boyd, hi. Sorry about the wait."

"No, it's my fault entirely. I just assumed you'd be up by now."

"I was, I was," I lied. "Completely awake."

Justin scrutinized my face and, after a moment, seemed to remember why he was there. "Our flight is leaving, and I just wanted to say goodbye in person. You were phenomenal yesterday and really, everyone was so impressed."

"Thank you, sir." That was when I noticed the two envelopes in his hand.

"This is for you." He handed me the envelope with my name on it, a bonus for performing well this weekend.

"Thank you, sir," I said again. "I really appreciate it, and the team has been great to work with. Dom is a fantastic captain to work for."

"Yes," he said a little distractedly. His eyes were looking over my shoulder and I prayed to God that Seb was still in the closet. I said a second prayer, hoping my underwear wasn't hanging conspicuously somewhere. Who knew where it had gotten tossed last night?

"I was looking for Seb, too. He wasn't in his cabin when I stopped by."

I froze and said the first thing that came to mind. "Maybe he went running?"

Justin gave me an odd look. "I think I'll just leave

his envelope with you, okay?" Justin handed me the envelope and leaned toward me. "Seb, thanks for the great job this weekend, yeah?"

My stomach plummeted.

"Thank you, sir," came Seb's muffled voice from the wardrobe. Justin nodded at the confirmation.

I closed my eyes, my stomach absolutely sinking to my feet, and pinched the bridge of my nose.

Justin chuckled under his breath. "See you next time, Marcella."

My eyes popped open in surprise, but Justin was already walking away. *See you next time*. What did that mean?

I closed the door and leaned back against it, sliding down to the floor. "Oh my God, oh my God, oh my God."

"Marcella?" Seb looked out from the wardrobe and his eyes widened when he saw me. He stepped out, wearing only a T-shirt with a skort from my uniform bunched in his hand. My eyes filled with tears.

"Hey," he crooned, approaching me as if I were a wild animal. "It's okay. It's going to be okay."

"No, it's not! I've just done a great job, I worked so hard these six weeks, and now Justin knows that we're sleeping together, and that's not good. I like this job; I don't want to look for a new one." I was crying now, tears of frustration trailing down my face. Why did I have to fuck this up again?

Seb crouched down beside me. "Marcella, it's going to be okay."

I looked at Seb and all of my anger balled up and spit itself out at him. "For God's sake, Seb, put some pants on."

His face hardened. "Excuse me, but the woman I just slept with—again—is on the floor crying. I'd be an asshole if I didn't check on you."

"So that was 'checking on me'? Letting our boss know that we're sleeping together? You might as well have walked out of the closet waving and inviting him to join us."

"What the fuck, Marce? I would never do that. Can we just back up a bit, please?" Bewildered, Seb ran his fingers through his hair and tugged.

I pushed him away from me. "Sure, yes, back up." I stood up and started to hunt for Seb's clothes. "Let's back way up. Back before we slept together." I threw his shorts at him.

"Marce, you were the one who invited me in last night. I would never come stay without your permission."

"Well, I was dumb." My voice was rising, frustration building in me. How could I have put myself in the same position? "I said I didn't want us to do this while Justin and Natasha were here. It was too risky, and now they know!"

"It wasn't dumb." Seb tried to grab my hand and stop my frantic search. I pulled away from him, the back of my legs hitting the bed and I slumped inelegantly against it.

"That's easy for you to say."

"You aren't going to lose your job over this." He tried to placate me.

"Would you have said that last time?"

This question stalled him. "What?"

"Last time. Last time we had sex, back on *Odyssey*. Did you think that I wasn't going to lose my job over it?"

"Wait." Seb's face was screwed up with confusion and he took a step back from me. "I don't understand."

"What part don't you understand?"

"You . . . you quit *Odyssey*."

"I did not."

"Marce, Captain Carl told me you quit."

"I didn't quit. I was fired because I was 'a distraction.' But he said . . . he said other things too, about how the boat was coming out of the water and I was overqualified if there weren't going to be charter guests. So, yeah, I was fired."

"Well, I wasn't fired. And honestly, I've never

heard of anyone getting fired for sleeping with a fellow crew member for just one night." He crouched down in front of me. "Honestly, Marce, he was just an ass."

I wiped the tears from my cheeks and Seb slid down farther onto the floor to his knees, his hands coming to rest on either side of me on the mattress. I wanted to feel relief, to know that it wasn't my fault and I didn't deserve that treatment. But I couldn't let go of the fear.

"Look." He sighed. "We've been doing great, and even though it's only been a few weeks, we should just see how this runs. We can't take back what Justin knows, and neither he nor Dom are the type to rag things out. If we're fired, we're fired. But I really doubt it. This isn't Carl, this isn't *Odyssey*. We're not even the same people we were back then."

My fingers toyed with the hem of my shirt. "You might be right, but this is my dream job." I looked over at Seb, and he was watching me. "It's not worth risking."

His eyes widened, and I steeled myself to keep going. "I really don't want to lose this job, so I think we should call it quits before our relationship gets in the way. It may already be too late. . . ." I trailed off and looked down at my lap.

"Marce, that's not . . . I know you are kind of new

to being a yachtie, but this can work, we can make it work."

I gritted my teeth. "You can't know that. We don't even have a public relationship, so it's, like . . . not real."

My words were sharp, and he flinched.

"You've heard Dom talk about relationships between yachties. This isn't going to work." I set my chin, more stubborn now and ready to stand my ground. "I am here for this job."

Seb stood up and paced away from me, the three steps it took to get to the other side of the room. He ran a hand through his hair and turned back. "Yachtie relationships work—we can get a couples job."

I crossed my arms over my chest. "How many couples have you worked with?"

"I don't know. A few. What about that American couple? Bryce and what's-her-name? We could get a job together like them."

"I don't want to leave *Themis*."

"Neither do I."

"I don't . . ." I closed my eyes briefly. "It's too complicated, Seb. Just leave it be, okay? It's not worth it."

"You mean I'm not worth it." He shuddered, his

head tipping forward and his chest rising on a big breath.

My stomach dropped. "That's not what I said. I think you're great. But this is my job. How many times can I uproot my life to try to find what I want?" My voice edged into begging.

"That's not what I'm asking for, Marce." His hands dropped to his sides, palms splayed out. "You fit in here. You've proven yourself, at least to Justin and Natasha and the rest of the crew. How can you prove yourself to *you*? And how can you ask me to give this up when you fit *me*?"

I took a ragged inhale as Seb spun and paced away.

"You think we can keep this on the down-low, but we can't. This isn't just something you sneak past other people. I've been in your bed nearly every night for weeks. We've been tiptoeing around and pretending this is something it's not."

He looked up, his eyes fierce and determined.

"This is not a fling for me. You were never a fling for me."

As still as a statue, he waited for something—anything—from me. But I didn't know how to respond to this. I didn't know what was safe anymore.

Seb groaned into my silence, wiping his hands

over his face. When he pulled away, he wouldn't look at me, and I couldn't take my eyes off him. I begged myself to think of something to say, something that didn't ruin my career, something that didn't irrevocably damage Seb—or me.

But I didn't have the magic words.

"Marce—" His voice broke. When I said nothing, Seb opened the door and stepped into the hallway.

Hand on the knob, he turned back to me, his face grave.

"I'll make sure you don't lose your job. In fact, I'll stay out of your way, out of your galley. You just . . . take care of yourself."

The door clicked shut, and I squeezed my eyes closed and pressed my forehead against it.

Seb was good at taking care of me. But I didn't know how to take care of myself.

THIRTY-ONE

"HEY, MARCE, CAN YOU COME UP TO THE HELM?" Dom's call came in over the intercom. It was the afternoon two days after Justin and Natasha had left. The yacht crew had been given two full days off, and I hadn't left my room much. Overhead, I'd been able to hear the sounds of the rest of the crew enjoying their days off—the rope swing was probably out again, and the Jet Skis had been zipping past—but I'd stayed in my room, quiet and moping. I wondered if Seb was outside with the rest of the crew.

Climbing the stairs up to the pilothouse, I replayed the fateful day on *Odyssey* when I'd been fired. Was this about to be a repeat?

When I knocked on the door, Dom called out for me to enter. The pilothouse was empty save Dom, and he gestured for me to sit in the chair next to him.

My heart was beating hard and fast while I climbed up into the chair and settled myself. I knitted my fingers together in my lap and tried to steady my breathing.

"Marcella," Dom began, "Justin told me about the . . . situation . . . he found you in on Monday morning."

A sour taste filled my mouth, and I shifted my weight in the chair, gripping the armrest. It might be best to say as little as possible. "Yes."

"If there is a relationship going on, I would like to be made aware of it—"

"There's no relationship," I interrupted. "It was just . . . It won't happen again." If I wasn't so scared of losing my job, I would have at least been mortified to be talking about my sex life with my boss.

Dom's eyebrows dropped, concern etched on his face. He ran his hand over his beard, scratching his chin. "Relationships on board are tough, and I know my experiences may be a little colored by—"

"No, really." I waved my hands, trying to come up with the words to assure Dom that it wasn't that big of a deal. "It's over, and we rarely see each other most days. I won't let it interfere with my job, or his."

"Marcella . . ." The way he said my name was full of sympathy and made my stomach flip. I gripped the armrests again.

"Am I fired?"

Dom shook his head. "No, you aren't fired. You worked hard, and the Boyds are impressed. I know it wasn't easy in the beginning, but there's a learning curve. Especially with Natasha." His lips tipped up at the joke. My response must have looked pathetic, because his eyebrows pinched together tighter.

"I hope you have realized by now that I value a work-life balance, and I expect my crew to have some fun."

"I do have fun," I insisted.

Dom cut me a look. "You have some fun, but you also clearly work harder than anyone else. And Seb's the kind of guy who would help you . . ."

He trailed off, and I fidgeted under his gaze. "I just want to keep things professional."

Shoulders sagging a bit, Dom nodded. "Fine, then, let's keep it professional. I do have a new contract for you to review here." He slipped a small stack of papers toward me.

I relaxed—a tiny bit.

"It's a one-year permanent contract with us now, the end of your probationary period. An increase in pay"—he circled a section with his pen—"and a few options for seasonal time off. Read it over and think about it. If there's anything you need to talk about, my door is always open to you." He spread his hands and shrugged.

"Thank you, Dom. You don't have to worry about this. I promise." I got up from the chair and left, a flood of relief passing through me. I was being given another chance, and I would not let Dom down.

LIFE MOVED ON, BACK TO NORMAL—EXCEPT FOR SEB. He avoided spending time in the galley, and when he would grab a bite to eat, he'd be short with Roy. He kept moving, passing through quickly and barely meeting my eyes. The latest quote had disappeared from the whiteboard, and I left the space blank.

At night I stared at the photograph of my great-grandparents, reminding myself that I had a goal, a job to do and a world to see. Despite these reminders, my heart ached terribly, missing Seb in bed with me every night.

Roy had not brought up Seb to me. Surely, he knew that things were over—Seb was coming back to their cabin every night now. Instead we focused on the upcoming schedule: a few charters in Spain, another visit from the Boyds, and then departing to sail across the Atlantic Ocean.

That last part had my nerves a little frayed, but

Roy had already made the trip twice before, and it was going to be nothing like the twenty-five-day crossing I'd done on *Eik*. *Themis* would blaze a path in ten days from Gibraltar to Antigua, where we would begin the Caribbean season. Some of the crew was leaving, their contracts up, and they were moving on to other things. I, thankfully, was staying. Justin and Natasha, after discussing the entire situation, had stood firm on their offer for my new contract. I'd be on *Themis* for a season island-hopping in the Caribbean, and then we'd spend hurricane season moving up the east coast of the United States. A company had been hired to help us all with our visas, and blocks of time had been dedicated for crew breaks.

There were even two regattas on the schedule, one in the Caribbean and one in Rhode Island. This time, *Themis* would compete in the races against other superyachts.

All I had to do was put my head down and work hard. Time would pass, Seb would eventually start coming into the galley—he had to eat, after all—and I'd grow more secure in my position. This could work. This could still be my dream job.

"This is the last pie." Roy slid the chicken-and-leek pastry out of the oven and onto the countertop. I shook myself out of my thoughts and back to the task at hand: prepping for our passage to Barcelona. It would take *Themis* nearly two days to make the passage, so we had twice as many meals to prep as last time. Roy and I had been at work baking all day, preparing for us to leave that night.

"Good, we have plenty of time to get dinner ready early for the crew before we leave." Our intended time of departure was seven in the evening, so we had an early dinner scheduled.

"Marce, you should take a break." He checked the clock. "We have plenty of time. You could go take a nap."

Just the thought of a nap was tempting, but I stifled my yawn and lied through my teeth. "I'm not tired."

Roy gripped the edges of the sink and dropped his head forward. His shoulders were tense, drawn up to his ears.

"Then go explore Malta or something. Marce, you've got to get out a little bit. You haven't taken a break in a week and, while I appreciate you giving me time off, I hate to say this, but you are cranky as hell."

I glared at him. "I am not."

"You are and you're being irresponsible. You are too tired, even if you don't want to admit it. I know you; I've worked alongside you now for how long?

Three months?" He pushed back from the sink and grabbed my hand. "This," he said, pointing to the plasters on my index and middle fingers. "This never would have happened to the chef I know."

I tugged my hands away from him and pulled out a fresh cutting board. "I can sleep on the passage. Let's keep going."

Roy let out a weary sigh and plucked out my chef's knife before I could touch it. "Fine, but no knives."

His glare refuted my arguments before they could start. "Fine," I conceded, and set to work.

THIRTY-TWO

I DID SLEEP LIKE THE DEAD ON THE WAY TO BARCELONA—for most of the trip. I woke in the early morning on our last day at sea and stared at the ceiling, rocking on my bed with the boat. *Themis* was moving more than I'd felt before, the room tilted, the waves splashing against the hull beside me.

My thoughts kept turning to Seb. When we'd had our night in Antigua, maybe getting immediately sacked had been for the best, because this time it had gone beyond one night and I felt obsessed. I couldn't stop thinking about him. Instead of a single hot night, we'd had so much more, and I ached.

A rumble emanated from my stomach and I peeled myself out of bed, grateful for a distraction. I dressed and walked toward the galley, bracing myself against the walls as *Themis* heeled over.

When we left Malta, Roy and I had put away as much as possible in the event of a rough ride like this one. But throughout the trip, other crew members had been in and out, and things weren't put away like they should be. An orange rolled against the leeward wall, dishware clattered together in the sink, and someone had spilled a white powder on the counter by the stove.

I bent over to pick up the orange and my stomach somersaulted. Uh-oh.

The queasiness set in quickly, and I needed fresh air before I heaved up bile. It rarely happened, but since I hadn't eaten in a day or so, my stomach and mind weren't in sync.

When I pushed the door from the crew lounge to the main deck open, a chilly wind blasted against me, banging the door open farther than I'd expected, and then the rocking of *Themis* slammed it shut behind me. It was gray—the sky, the rain, the ocean, the spray. Belatedly, I realized the fastest way outside was the worst one. I was on the bow of *Themis*, subject to the elements and ill prepared. I turned to grip the door handle, slippery in my hands, and tried to pull the door open.

"Marce!"

I looked up at the shout, and a hooded figure fell

on top of me, shielding me as a wave crashed over our bow.

Seb.

He was dressed in his foul-weather gear, waterproof pants and a rain jacket. His arms came around me, grabbing the handle of the door and bracing us for the spray of water. The fat drops of ocean slapped Seb's clothes and stung our hands.

Seb pulled the door open and then shoved me inside. The door slammed shut behind us, sealing us off from the world. The noises vanished, an eerie, artificial calm in the eye of the storm.

"What. The. Fuck. Marce!"

I closed my eyes, taking a deep breath and pushing now damp tendrils of hair away from my face. When I brushed the water from my eyes and opened them again, Seb was beet red, eyes enraged and furious.

And then *Themis* heaved under my feet again. This time, I gave in to my stomach, and quickly pulled out the trash bin from under the sink and kneeled. My mouth opened, but nothing came out.

Behind me, Seb sighed. "Oh, flaquita." His fingers wrapped around my upper arm; a palm brushed my hair back from my forehead.

I stared at the trash in the bin, the apple core and

crinkled bags and wrappers as Seb rubbed my shoulders.

Nothing happened for a few moments and I sat back on my heels.

"Have you eaten?"

I shook my head.

"Okay. Let's get you up to the helm. You'll be more comfortable up there and I'll get you some food."

Taking my elbow, Seb guided me through the dining room and up the atrium. I leaned gratefully on him, even though the feel of his body, the heat of his skin, was also a different kind of torture.

"Look who we've got to join the party," Seb called out as he opened the helm door. Dom stood by one of the instrument stations, travel mug in hand, chatting with Will, who was curled up in one of the armchairs.

Upon seeing me, Dom's brow etched in concern. "Marcella? Are you not feeling well?"

Seb answered for me while helping me up into one of the other chairs. "She hasn't eaten. I'm going to grab something for her. Marcella, keep your eyes on the horizon, okay?"

"I know." It came out short and curt, ungrateful, and I didn't mean it that way. He reacted, a subtle tightening of his jaw and lips.

"Right, I'll be back."

In the chair, I buried my head in my hands and then immediately regretted it. I trained my eyes out on the horizon, and Dom puttered around the helm, adjusting a fan to point on my face and then throwing a blanket over my shoulders.

"It always gets cold up here," he commented.

I thanked him but kept looking at the sky. I tried to relax. With the air moving around me, and the view, I felt better. Better enough to feel foolish for stepping out in the first place and for the way I'd treated Seb.

He returned with some ginger biscuits and soda.

"Thanks," I whispered.

His eyes held mine and it was the first time we had looked at each other—*really* looked at each other—since the incident with Justin. What I saw took my breath away. I'd expected and deserved anger, but instead I was met with warmth, sadness, and something so tender, I couldn't . . .

Seb turned away, and after a few hushed words with Dom, left the three of us alone on the bridge deck.

I replayed the scene over and over again. How foolish it had been to step outside. Seb should have been angry with me, but he'd been his unflappable self, taking care of me when I needed it. Despite the fact that I'd hurt him, twice now, he was here. He still looked at me like that, without condition, and I realized I had made a mistake.

This job might have conditions, but Seb didn't give me any. And I shouldn't be giving him any either.

I gripped the snacks tightly in my fists.

"Dom," I said, "I'm in love with Seb."

He choked on his breath, coughing and pounding his chest. When he regained his composure, he took a deep breath in. He braced himself on the counter, his eyes full of sympathy. "Marcella, Seb gave me his notice."

I CLIMBED THE STAIRS UP TO THE BRIDGE DECK, ROY right behind me. We carried lunch service for three—sandwiches for me, Dom, and a guest.

After my confession, Dom had asked for patience. And then he'd scheduled a meeting for us.

Roy and I stepped out onto the aft deck, where Dom sat at the patio with a woman dressed in a pantsuit. Her hair was swept back into a slick ponytail, shot through with gray, and I guessed she was in her fifties.

Dom spotted me. "Marcella, come join us." He

waved me in. "This is Nilda. She's one of the best yacht placement agents in the Med, and she is based here in Barcelona."

As I approached the table, Nilda rose and offered me her hand. I set the platters on the table and shook it while Roy put down the place settings.

"Pleased to meet you." Nilda's accent was thick and local.

"Nice to meet you too," I said nervously. I slid into one of the empty seats and crossed my legs. Roy squeezed my shoulder before exiting. Why would I need to speak to a staffing agent?

"Marcella," Dom began, "I fear I have not been very supportive of you recently, and I may have let my personal thoughts on the matter sour your viewpoint."

"What matter are you referring to?"

"Relationships among the yachties."

My eyes flicked over to Nilda and then dropped.

Dom continued. "Nilda is an expert in placing couples in crew positions."

"I am." Nilda nodded at me with a soft smile. "Dom tells me you are relatively new to the superyacht industry, and I think we need to clear up some things."

I swallowed. "I'm listening."

"I actually place a lot more couples than I do

singles now. It used to not be the case, but when you market it right, couples can have an extreme advantage on yacht jobs. Couples tend to be more reliable, they support each other, and when they've been together a fairly long time, they are seen as more stable than younger, single staff.

"You have a few unique things going for you. You are more experienced in your field, at the top tier, if what I've heard from Dom and Natasha is right."

It took a minute for Nilda's words to register. "Natasha?"

"Yes. Dom and I had a discussion with her and Justin and they were both on board with this conversation. I've placed chefs for Natasha before, and she's extremely particular. I know she's not easy to work for."

My lips tilted up at the understatement and I had to hold back a laugh. I had never worked for someone so difficult—or rewarding—in my life.

Nilda waved a hand to move the discussion along. "So, placing you in the perfect job is hard because you are too qualified, and there's a slim number of owners who look for your level of quality. I don't mean this as a bad thing, but Seb's job is the opposite. He's younger, gaining experience and working up the ranks. Any yacht that is looking for a chef like you likely has a place for Seb."

"We aren't saying that finding two perfect jobs on the same boat is an easy thing," Dom clarified. "But it is possible."

"Sixty percent of the positions I placed last year were couples," Nilda told me proudly. "And based on my personal experience, they have lasted longer in the positions I've placed them in over people who are single."

"Okay," I said. "All this makes sense, and I appreciate the clarification. But . . . Seb quit."

Nilda chuckled under her breath and Dom shifted in his seat, embarrassed. "He didn't exactly quit yet. I kind of refused to accept his resignation. And the, um, argument after that led to me calling Nilda in to talk to you."

My eyebrows pulled together. "So you want Nilda to find us new jobs?"

"No. I want you both to stay, but with us all in agreement that you are a couple, and if one of you leaves or gets let go, the other is likely to leave. We just need to communicate better about these things."

"This is like an HR policy discussion." Nilda laughed. "I'm the HR manager, and I won't make you sign anything, but perhaps you will feel like you can have a talk with Seb?"

I looked to Dom, who held out his hands. "No pressure on my part. If you want Seb to stay, I think you just have to ask him. I hate to lose him, but I understand his viewpoint. And, Marcella . . ." He cleared his throat. "I am really sorry that I've made you worry about your job so much. I know yachties sleep around or fall in love, it's inevitable, and just because I didn't have a good experience with my ex doesn't mean you shouldn't be happy if Seb is who you want."

Nilda spread her hands out. "So, Marcella, what do you think?"

The pragmatic part of me thought it sounded too good to be true. But the rest of me, the hopeful part of me who loved Seb, knew that it was worth a try. I would try anything.

For the first time since Seb and I had broken up, I laughed. "Yes, this is what I want."

THIRTY-THREE

I RETURNED DOWNSTAIRS TO THE GALLEY, MY HEAD spinning. I was keeping my job and I had my boss's blessing to . . . have an official relationship. Roy put his knife down when he saw me, and braced himself on the counter. "So?" he asked. "Is everything okay?"

"Yeah," I said, bewildered. On autopilot, I got back to work.

I picked back up chopping vegetables for dinner service, and let my brain mull things over while I diced. Then Roy plunked down next to me.

"What *are* you doing?"

I blinked and focused my eyes. I'd been staring at the cutting board without actually cutting anything for several minutes. I blinked more, trying to ease the sting of dry eyes that had been staring off into space.

"I'm thinking."

Roy picked up a whole carrot and brandished it at me. "And cutting vegetables with your laser eyesight?"

I blushed. "No."

"You know Seb's waiting for you, right?"

"He is?"

"Yes. And maybe the rest of the crew is too."

I gave Roy a look and he shrugged at me.

"It's pretty obvious what's going on here. I didn't have to say anything; my lips were sealed. It's the way you two look at each other. At first it was all 'sexual tension' and being rumpled and then it was making gooey eyes at each other. And now you've been moping."

The knife dropped from my hand and clattered onto the counter. "I've been an idiot."

"Yes."

"I didn't know!" I wailed.

"What, that yachties are sex fiends? Totally."

"Roy! Who are you a sex fiend with?"

"Nuh-uh." He waggled a finger at me. "Less talk about me. Less talk *to* me. Go and talk to Seb. Please."

I bit my lip. "He quit."

Roy's head tilted. "Derick renewed his contract, so Seb has no room for advancement here. And that does bite . . . but he would have *you*."

"You think Seb would stay just for me?"

His eyes turned tender. Wordlessly, he pointed to the whiteboard.

Written in the blank space, in Seb's handwriting: *"After a good dinner, one can forgive anybody." —Oscar Wilde*

I pursed my lips. "Actually, I have a better idea. What are we serving tomorrow?"

WHEN THE DOOR TO THE CREW QUARTERS OPENED, I WAS ready.

Roy said, "Go ahead," and Seb responded with a "Thanks, man." Seb stepped into the lounge and the door closed behind him. He glanced back, surprised, but then he caught sight of me.

"Hi," I started nervously.

Seb looked around the galley. "Hey, yourself. I thought you'd have the day off today?"

I shook my head. "I gave Roy the day off."

An eyebrow rose. "You got Roy to wake up early on his day off?"

"He's surprisingly romantic." I shrugged.

Seb stepped forward and placed his hands on the counter, leaning toward me. "And what is so romantic about today?"

I mirrored him, leaning against the other side of the island. "I made a special day today, just for you. First, we have Italian coffee." I turned around and pointed to the tray of freshly baked guava pastries. "I tried to find some Cuban *pastelitos* to make you, but there wasn't much I could work with. But these have guava on the inside." Seb walked around the island and picked up a pastry. "And I couldn't find Cuban bread, either, of course, so I put baguettes on the sandwich press."

Seb looked up, watching me.

"There's meat cooking in the oven to make *ropa vieja* today. And then *medianoche* sandwiches for dinner."

The corner of his mouth twitched. "And then flan?"

"Of course."

He leaned back against the counter, arms straight and tensed. "What does this mean, Marce? Why do this?"

"Because," I said quietly, "I want you to know how much you mean to me. I know I've hurt you twice, and you don't deserve that. You are the best man I've ever met. And we do fit together."

His steady gaze watched me.

"I know I work myself too hard and get run-down. And I worry about my job too much. And I'm still scared. All of these things are me, and I know I need to work on them myself, but also . . . I have faith in you. I feel more confident with you."

Seb straightened, his hand running through his curls, a breath of air leaving his lips. But then he leaned toward me, bracing his hip on the counter.

"Seb. I'm sorry." I stared up into his eyes, his expression serious. "I thought it would be a big ugly thing if we got caught, and I panicked because I can't seem to keep away from you. I was scared, and I'm sorry."

I watched, moment by moment, as Seb melted, his shoulders dropping and his mouth relaxing. He smiled softly. "I forgive you."

"You do?" A weight lifted, hope flooding in and encouraging me. Seb took the two steps around the counter toward me. He tilted his head down, looking into my eyes. "You'll get scared again, I know. And that's okay. But we can be a team, a really good one. You're the team I want."

He reached up and threaded his fingers through my hair before pulling me in for a deep kiss. My hands came up around his back to grip his shoulders and I opened up for him. His lips were warm and soft and I took a deep breath in, filling myself with the delicious way he smelled.

He pulled back slightly and nipped my lips as he ran his thumbs down my neck.

I panted under him, trying to catch my breath. His smile pressed into mine, and he took an inhale. "Fresh herbs and roasting meat and Marcella. It smells like home," he said, a twinkle in his eye. "What's the rest of the crew going to eat?" he teased.

"Ah well, I had to make enough for everybody since I gave Roy the day off and took over the menu for the day."

Seb started to step away, but I gripped his shirt and kept him in place.

"I didn't even tell you the best part."

Seb moved to the side, kissing his way down my neck and pressing us together harder. "What's the best part?" he murmured.

"So, apparently, we can stay on *Themis* together, as a team. If you want. To be with me, I mean." I cleared my throat.

His lips twitched up. "I do want to be with you. Here on *Themis*."

I licked my lips, my heart pounding in my chest. "Even if you stay on as a deckhand? I know you've really racked up your sea time on *Themis,* and you could have a better job, a bosun's job, elsewhere. I don't want you to resent me."

"I won't," he promised. "Dom's a great captain

to work under, and I'd still be getting plenty of sailing opportunities to pad my CV." He pressed his forehead to mine. "I'm still working on my goals. But I'm working on yours, too. A team, remember?"

"Yes, a team." I nodded. "We are a team. Because I love you."

Now his smile was full-blown, the corners of his eyes wrinkling. "I love you too, Marcella."

My stomach fluttered as Seb pulled me close again, and I wrapped my arms around his neck and enjoyed a deep kiss.

When I had arrived in Tivat, so hopeful to start my new job, I never would have imagined this was possible. Here I stood, with a wonderful career, memories of exploring multiple countries, and the thing I hadn't known I was missing—the support of a man like Seb.

The door cracked open behind me and a throat cleared. "Do I get to come in now?" Roy whispered.

Seb broke away, laughing, and I rolled my eyes. "Yes, come in, get a pastry."

Instead of beelining for the platter, Roy wrapped me up in a hug. "I'm glad you are staying." He let go of me and offered open arms to Seb, too. "I'm really glad you're staying. Sounds like I'll have a room to myself now."

Seb tugged me toward the exit. "You got this, Roy?"

"Wait, what?" Roy's face fell. "You don't want a coffee? Pastry? Hey, Marcella, how long does the beef need to cook?!" The door slammed on his last word and Seb pulled me down the hall.

"Where are we going?"

He grinned wickedly at me. "Makeup sex, of course."

EPILOGUE

THEMIS CUT OUT ALONG THE WIDE-OPEN OCEAN. WE'D been sailing for nine days now since we'd left Gibraltar, bound for Antigua. There was nothing but blue all around: sky and sea, two halves of the whole world surrounding us.

Will and I were on the bridge deck just outside of Justin and Natasha's room, doing some very basic yoga poses while *Themis* rocked gently underneath us. I thought about the big ocean passage I'd done on *Eik* and how exhausting it had been. This time, there were no watch obligations, *Themis* was an incredibly smooth ride, and we had eight of us spread out over the ninety-meter ship. It was hard to feel stir-crazy when you had so much room, even on a small dot in the middle of the Atlantic Ocean.

We had fewer crew than normal, since we were sailing *Themis* across an ocean. Some of the crew who were not staying on to next season were already gone. A few, like Roy, had opted to fly home for a break before flying to meet the boat in the Caribbean and begin the winter season.

"And into triangle pose," Will intoned beside me. We slid our right hands down to the floor, but kept the left pressed against a chair we'd repurposed to help us hold our balance out on the sea. A modified triangle pose.

"And kick back, *chaturanga dandasana* . . ." I let go of the chair, planting my hand on the floor and sliding my leg back into a push-up position. *Themis* rolled a bit, but I was much more stable.

Will and I worked through our routine until we lay on the floor. I closed my eyes, and the boat swung one way then the other underneath me.

"Ah, my favorite pose."

I peeked an eye open and found Seb watching me with a grin.

"It's not your favorite pose."

"Well, corpse pose is my favorite pose to *do*. But you are right: my favorite pose when you do yoga is anything where you bend over. Earmuffs, Will."

My yoga buddy grunted. "Fuck off, Seb. Ask nicely and I'll give you the entire room."

"Please."

Will turned his head to me. "See ya in the galley, Marce."

He vanished in a flash and Seb sat down next to me on the floor. "Do you always have to scare my yoga buddy off?"

"He likes an excuse to leave."

"One of these days I'll be making you do yoga with me again." Seb had tried it a few times while we were out at sea but declared it a bit too boring.

I rolled over, putting my head in his lap. "How was your watch?"

"Good. Absolutely nothing to report, just the way I like it."

We had six crew members doing shifts and two of us for the interior. Will handled most of the stew responsibilities, mostly just making sure people cleaned up after themselves and didn't make a total mess of the galley. I still handled the crew meals. Feeding the eight of us every day was easy, and in my spare time I was deep-cleaning the facilities and finding all kinds of interesting forgotten-but-still-good ingredients to use up.

"What's our latest ETA?" I asked Seb.

He shifted next to me, sprawling out on the floor and closing his eyes. "Tomorrow around noon."

"I can't believe we're coming back to Antigua, where we first met."

I could hear the grin in Seb's voice. "Sure, I remember you seeing me for the first time."

"Ha."

He propped himself up on an elbow. "I'm happy to re-create it tonight. If you walk into the cabin at exactly"—he looked at his watch and frowned in mock concentration—"6:53 p.m., I'll make sure to be stepping out of the shower"—he leaned toward my ear—"soaking wet, and well, it may not be an exact re-creation, because I'll probably be hard just thinking about you walking in—"

I shoved him away from me with a laugh. His smile was wide and happy, his eyes dancing in mirth as he took in my blush.

I WAS THE LAST ONE UP ON DECK AFTER BREAKFAST THE next morning. Most times I set out breakfast and people came and went as they pleased, but today was our last morning, so I took orders and made everyone a hot meal. Since we could now see the islands and the weather was sunny and beautiful, the crew was out on deck, dining alfresco.

As I climbed the stairs, I juggled my plate and my

mug of coffee and battled with the desire to look up. *Themis* was in all her glory, fully rigged and moving at a fast clip. We were sailing so well, we'd be getting in earlier than expected.

Seb spotted me and pulled out a chair next to him. As soon as my plate was down, my eyes snapped around, taking it all in. To our port side was Antigua, the island rocky and green. We were just a few kilometers away, having made our turn and sailing down the west coast of the island.

I spun around. On our starboard was Montserrat, and as I looked out beyond her, toward *Themis*'s stern, I saw St. Martin.

Seb squeezed my thigh when I sat down. "Almost there."

"Did you ever go to Montserrat?"

He shook his head.

Dom spoke up from across the table. "I haven't been, but it doesn't have a very good harbor. No docks, certainly not big enough for us anyway."

"I've been," Gio announced. "It's an active volcano. Pretty rugged, a hell of a hike."

"Did you like it?" I asked.

He shrugged. "Cute town, small as hell and not much to see."

"Hey, Marce," Seb interrupted. "That must be Jolly Harbour, where we were anchored last year."

Sure enough, we could see all the sailboats anchored, and even a big superyacht. We glanced at each other and burst out laughing. "Not *Odyssey,* thank God."

"No, but it looks pretty similar. I was almost scared for a minute."

We weren't staying in Jolly Harbour this time. Instead *Themis* was sailing to the bottom of Antigua and docking at Falmouth Harbour. It was a deep bay, with a marina big enough to fit a nice collection of superyachts. And it was well protected, with hills and forts all around. Jolly Harbour was more popular with the small sailboats, with its bigger grocery stores, cleaner water, and a stunning view of sunset. But it was too small for *Themis*.

My breakfast plate empty, I spun around in my chair and watched Montserrat pass by. When we'd been in Antigua on *Odyssey,* Montserrat had taunted me. I was supposed to be on a grand adventure sailing the islands, and instead I was confined on a yacht that was going nowhere. No charters, no guests, and no exploring.

Now I was coming back less than a year later, having sailed from Antigua to Tahiti, flying from Tahiti to Montenegro, and sailing back to Antigua. Pride rushed through my veins. When getting to the next island over had seemed impossible, I'd made something else happen, and gone around the world.

"What's so special about Montserrat?" Seb leaned onto my shoulder and kissed my skin, warm from the sun.

"I remember staring from *Odyssey* and wanting so badly to be anywhere else, exploring. And you, you were desperate for more sea time or a big crossing. And now look how far we've come."

Seb wrapped his arms around my shoulders. "I'm proud of us."

This visit to Antigua would be different. We weren't being held back anymore, and now we'd tackle it as a team.

IT TOOK US A FEW DAYS TO GET SETTLED INTO Falmouth. *Themis* got a good scrub down, I finished my deep clean of the galley, and the boat was aired out. I'd also met with my provisioning suppliers here and walked the shops looking for specific things I knew I would need to pick up for the arrival of the crew and the first charter of the season.

When I came back from a shopping trip, I stepped into the galley and found two duffel bags packed on the counter.

"What is this?" I wondered aloud.

"I packed your bag for you for an overnight trip." Seb stood in the doorway to the stairs. "We have a flight in two hours."

I blinked at him. "What? Where are we going?"

He stepped forward, bringing his hands up to relieve me of the grocery bags, then set them on the counter before wrapping his arms around me.

"We have a room booked for one night with a stunning view, and a fifteen-minute flight—yes, fifteen minutes—from the Antigua airport to Montserrat's airport."

I pulled back, surprised. "We're going to Montserrat?"

Seb bit his lip and nodded. "If you want."

"I want. How . . . What . . ." My mind focused on the most exciting part of that news. "We have two days off?"

Seb laughed. "Yes, two days off. And you know what this means?" He grabbed my hands and bounced them excitedly. "We get an actual date—"

"You took me on our first date in Gibraltar." Actually, it had been a whole day. We'd hiked to the top of the Rock, taking in the glorious views of the city and the emerald waters. Afterward, we'd scrambled back to *Themis,* hot and sweaty, to shower and dress before dining at a chef's table in Catalan Bay.

"—and a vacation together—"

"I think our life is a vacation together."

"—and a very big bed to share tonight." He preemptively cut me off with a kiss before I could say anything else, but there was nothing left to say. While my cabin was bigger than his, the room was still small, and our bed was tight with two people. Seb had officially moved into my—our—room in Gibraltar.

Seb kept his face close to mine, forehead touching while he brushed kisses against my lips. "A big bed will be nice," I conceded. "And Dom said it's okay?"

"Mm-hmm. Said taking two days off after a long passage was totally fine, and the crew can fend for themselves on takeout and sandwiches for a few days. And we will get to go hiking and have a great view and a romantic dinner."

I tilted my head back a bit. "This island will be ours."

Seb gave a firm nod. "Ours."

"We get to make all these new memories here in Antigua, replace the old ones and enjoy the island. But we're still here with our crews, our boat. Monserrat is a clean slate. It's only us."

"Only us," he echoed, a smirk on his lips.

"Wow, Seb." I stretched my arms up, wrapping them around his neck and pulling us even closer. "I just don't know what I'm going to do when I have you all to myself for two days."

"I have a list. Let's start with number one." And he kissed me, deeply and soundly.

THE END

Thank you for reading.
Subscribers to my newsletter get special content:

—the first chance prequel short story for Marcella and Seb

—photos and stories from my own trips that inspired the Love and Wanderlust series

Sign up for my emails at lizalden.com.

Please Review

Reviews are critical to all authors. You can leave a review for *The Second Chance in the Mediterranean* at all retailers

Amazon | Apple | Kobo

Barnes & Noble | Google Books

and

Goodreads | BookBub

Also by Liz Alden:

The Love and Wanderlust Series

The Night in Lover's Bay (prequel short story)

The Hitchhiker in Panama

The Sailor in Polynesia

The Second Chance in the Mediterranean

The Rival in South Africa (a novella in the *Hate Me Like You Mean It* anthology)

ACKNOWLEDGMENTS

I didn't intend to write this novel. This third book was supposed to be Claire's story of falling in love with a washed-up Māori rugby player. But Marcella was insistent that I wasn't done on the water yet, and she took me exploring the world of superyachts and the islands of the Mediterranean. And Seb . . . is a gem. I am so glad I wrote him.

Thank you to my advanced reader team. Their love for Eivind and Lila and Jonas and Mia helped keep me going, even in the worst of the revisions.

To my critique partners: Emy, Dani, Jeanine, and Katherine. I am always honored to have found such excellent support for my work when it is at its worst.

Thank you to my editors: Tiffany, who continues to coach me and turn me into a better writer, especially focusing on making my characters better people; Kaitlin, who polished this book like crazy; and Annette, who did the proofread.

Thank you to my cover designer, Elizabeth, who brings my characters to life.

To my husband, there is a bit of you in every one of my heroes, and that's what makes them so good.

ABOUT THE AUTHOR

Liz Alden is a digital nomad. Most of the time she's on her sailboat, but sometimes she's in Texas. She knows exactly how big the world is—having sailed around it—and exactly how small it is, having bumped into friends worldwide.

She's been a dishwasher, an engineer, a CEO, and occasionally gets paid to write or sail.

The Second Chance in the Mediterranean is her third novel.

For 100-word flash fiction stories, book reviews, and teasers for the Love and Wanderlust series, follow Liz.

lizalden.com

Made in the USA
Middletown, DE
16 January 2022

58849178R00189